CAN SUCH THINGS BE?

CAN SUCH THINGS BE?

Ambrose Bierce

WORDSWORTH AMERICAN LIBRARY

This edition published 1997 by
Wordsworth Editions Limited
Cumberland House, Crib Street
Ware, Hertfordshire SG12 9ET

ISBN 1 85326 570 5

Typeset by Antony Gray
Printed and bound in Great Britain by
Mackays of Chatham plc, Chatham, Kent

INTRODUCTION

Ambrose Bierce (1842–1914), most of whose work appeared in San Francisco periodicals, was recognised in his own time as a skilled and influential journalist, the terror of corrupt politicians and unscrupulous magnates in northern California as well as of vainglorious poetasters. But he was also a writer of short stories, poems, and the witty barbs to be found in *The Devil's Dictionary* that are still current today and that illuminate some of the tales printed here. For example, the nineteenth-century practice of medical students' robbing graves to get cadavers for their studies lies behind both his definition of GRAVE as 'A place in which the dead are laid to await the coming of the medical student' and the story 'One Summer Night'. 'A Tough Tussle' conforms almost exactly to his definition of GHOST as 'The outward and visible sign of an inward fear.'

Can Such Things Be? is not as well known as his earlier *In the Midst of Life*, but he gave a good deal of thought to the assignment of his stories to these two volumes in succeeding editions, sometimes to one book, sometimes to the other. Those reprinted here represent his final allocation of tales to *Can Such Things Be?* in 1910. 'The Haunted Valley', his earliest short story, was first published in the *Overland Monthly* in July 1871 and is not one of his better efforts. Nevertheless, the extensive revisions he made to it before its final publication show how his craftsmanship had developed with the passage of years. However, of all the tales in this volume, the most discussed among scholars today is 'The Death of Halpin Frayser', although it is still not as well known to the general public as 'An Occurrence at Owl Creek Bridge'. Theories to account for its mysteries abound, some of them supernatural, some not.

To put the stories collected here in their historical context, one needs to know that paranormal phenomena were the subject of serious investigation by some of the best minds of the late nineteenth century. In 1882 the Society for Psychical Research was established in England, where Bierce had lived from 1872 to 1875. One of its founders was the philosopher Henry Sidgwick, and William James was in the thick of its investigations. It published classified reports of hundred of ghosts and listed in its *Proceedings* those mediums who could allegedly transmit messages from the dead. In the United States the philosopher Josiah Royce, who like Bierce early in his career wrote for the *Overland Monthly*, contributed a number of items to the *Proceedings of the American Society for Psychical Research* from 1886 to 1889; and he was chairman of its Committee on Phantasms and Presentiments.

Even the sceptical Bierce took seriously the endeavours of both these societies. He revealed in the New York *Journal* for 25 April 1901 that he had once been approached by the American Society for authenticating evidence concerning his own highly circumstantial ghost stories, and he urged his readers to co-operate with the Society in its requests for information, commenting that 'the question of human immortality is the most momentous that the mind is capable of conceiving. If it is a fact that the dead live, all other facts are in comparison trivial and without interest.'

He uses a medium, Bayrolles, in two of the stories in *Can Such Things Be?*: 'The Moonlit Road' and 'An Inhabitant of Carcosa'. In 'One of Twins' the narrator is responding to someone doing 'psychological researches' who has asked him whether he had 'ever observed anything unaccountable by the natural laws with which we have acquaintance'. A character in 'The Damned Thing' says: 'We so rely upon the orderly operation of familiar natural laws that any seeming suspension of them is noted as a menace to our safety, a warning of unthinkable calamity.' He then suggests that the deadly invisible creature that had killed a friend of his may have been made up of colours beyond the range of perception by human eyes. In both 'The Death of Halpin Frayser' and 'An Inhabitant of Carcosa', Bierce refers to writings of Altaf Husain Hali (1837–1914), an Urdu poet, prose writer and critic.

Attempts to place the contents of this volume under the rubrics of 'the supernatural' or 'science fiction' may not hold up, since such classifications depend on particular interpretations of the stories. Other interpretations may take them out of these categories. For example, 'Moxon's Master' may or may not be science fiction, depending on one's interpretation. 'A Tough Tussle', too, is not so much explicitly supernatural as it is an account of the hereditary influence the mere fact of death can have on a sensitive mind. And 'A Resumed Identity' could be interpreted as exemplifying an extended case of amnesia. In this story Bierce, who had served four years in the Civil War, includes the

actual military phenomenon of 'acoustic shadows', or what have been
called 'silent battles', as at Chancellorsville, where sounds inaudible to
persons a short distance from the source may be heard over a hundred
miles away in another direction.

'Haïta the Shepherd' is a didactic tale about the pursuit of happiness,
symbolised as a beautiful woman; she comes to those who are truthful
and do their duty, but who do not worship her, for she is not a goddess.
But if we avoid the term 'supernatural' for the remaining stories in this
volume, which are mimetic, we might call them 'uncanny'. The fact
that the influence of Freud has had its day should not blind us to the
fact that certain insights can still be gleaned from some of his writings.
Thus, without accepting all his conclusions, one can read his essay
'The Uncanny' with profit in connection with *Can Such Things Be?* In
the last analysis, however, the best guidance to this book was given us
by Bierce himself in his title. It is taken from *Macbeth*, III, iv, 110–12:

> Can such things be,
> And overcome us like a summer's cloud,
> Without our special wonder?

M. E. GRENANDER
The University at Albany
State University of New York

FURTHER READING

Lawrence I. Berkove (ed.), *Ambrose Bierce, Skepticism and Dissent*,
Delmas, Ann Arbor, Michigan 1980

Cathy N. Davidson (ed.), *Critical Essays on Ambrose Bierce*, Hall,
Boston 1982

Cathy N. Davidson, *The Experimental Fictions of Ambrose Bierce:
Structuring the Ineffable*, University of Nebraska Press,
Lincoln 1984

M. E. Grenander, *Ambrose Bierce*, Twayne, New York 1971

M. E. Grenander, 'Ambrose Bierce', *Dictionary of Literary Biography*,
volumes 12 and 71, Gale, Detroit, Michigan 1982 and 1988

M. E. Grenander (ed.), *Poems of Ambrose Bierce*, University of
Nebraska Press, Lincoln 1995

CONTENTS

CAN SUCH THINGS BE?

The Death of Halpin Frayser

⚜ ONE ⚜

For by death is wrought greater change than hath been
shown. Whereas in general the spirit that removed cometh
back upon occasion, and is sometimes seen of those in flesh
(appearing in the form of the body it bore) yet it hath
happened that the veritable body without the spirit hath
walked. And it is attested of those encountering who have
lived to speak thereon that a lich so raised up hath no
natural affection, nor remembrance thereof, but only hate.
Also, it is known that some spirits which in life were benign
become by death evil altogether.   HALL

One dark night in midsummer a man waking from a dreamless sleep in
a forest lifted his head from the earth, and staring a few moments into
the blackness, said: 'Catharine Larue.' He said nothing more; no
reason was known to him why he should have said so much.

The man was Halpin Frayser. He lived in St Helena, but where he
lives now is uncertain, for he is dead. One who practises sleeping in the
woods with nothing under him but the dry leaves and the damp earth,
and nothing over him but the branches from which the leaves have
fallen and the sky from which the earth has fallen, cannot hope for
great longevity, and Frayser had already attained the age of thirty-two.
There are persons in this world, millions of persons, and far and away
the best persons, who regard that as a very advanced age. They are the
children. To those who view the voyage of life from the port of
departure the bark that has accomplished any considerable distance
appears already in close approach to the farther shore. However, it is
not certain that Halpin Frayser came to his death by exposure.

He had been all day in the hills west of the Napa Valley, looking for doves and such small game as was in season. Late in the afternoon it had come on to be cloudy, and he had lost his bearings; and although he had only to go always downhill – everywhere the way to safety when one is lost – the absence of trails had so impeded him that he was overtaken by night while still in the forest. Unable in the darkness to penetrate the thickets of manzanita and other undergrowth, utterly bewildered and overcome with fatigue, he had lain down near the root of a large madroño and fallen into a dreamless sleep. It was hours later, in the very middle of the night, that one of God's mysterious messengers, gliding ahead of the incalculable host of his companions sweeping westward with the dawn line, pronounced the awakening word in the ear of the sleeper, who sat upright and spoke, he knew not why, a name, he knew not whose.

Halpin Frayser was not much of a philosopher, nor a scientist. The circumstance that, waking from a deep sleep at night in the midst of a forest, he had spoken aloud a name that he had not in memory and hardly had in mind did not arouse an enlightened curiosity to investigate the phenomenon. He thought it odd, and with a little perfunctory shiver, as if in deference to a seasonal presumption that the night was chill, he lay down again and went to sleep. But his sleep was no longer dreamless.

He thought he was walking along a dusty road that showed white in the gathering darkness of a summer night. Whence and whither it led, and why he travelled it, he did not know, though all seemed simple and natural, as is the way in dreams; for in the Land Beyond the Bed surprises cease from troubling and the judgement is at rest. Soon he came to a parting of the ways; leading from the highway was a road less travelled, having the appearance, indeed, of having been long abandoned, because, he thought, it led to something evil; yet he turned into it without hesitation, impelled by some imperious necessity.

As he pressed forward he became conscious that his way was haunted by invisible existences whom he could not definitely figure to his mind. From among the trees on either side he caught broken and incoherent whispers in a strange tongue which yet he partly understood. They seemed to him fragmentary utterances of a monstrous conspiracy against his body and soul.

It was now long after nightfall, yet the interminable forest through which he journeyed was lit with a wan glimmer having no point of diffusion, for in its mysterious lumination nothing cast a shadow. A shallow pool in the guttered depression of an old wheel rut, as from a recent rain, met his eye with a crimson gleam. He stooped and plunged his hand into it. It stained his fingers; it was blood! Blood, he then observed, was about him everywhere. The weeds growing rankly by the roadside showed it in blots and plashes on their big, broad leaves. Patches of dry dust between the wheel-ways were pitted and spattered as with a red rain. Defiling the trunks of the trees were broad maculations of crimson, and blood dripped like dew from their foliage.

All this he observed with a terror which seemed not incompatible with the fulfilment of a natural expectation. It seemed to him that it was all in expiation of some crime which, though conscious of his guilt, he could not rightly remember. To the menaces and mysteries of his surroundings the consciousness was an added horror. Vainly he sought, by tracing life backward in memory, to reproduce the moment of his sin; scenes and incidents came crowding tumultuously into his mind, one picture effacing another, or commingling with it in confusion and obscurity, but nowhere could he catch a glimpse of what he sought. The failure augmented his terror; he felt as one who has murdered in the dark, not knowing whom nor why. So frightful was the situation – the mysterious light burned with so silent and awful a menace; the noxious plants, the trees that by common consent are invested with a melancholy or baleful character, so openly in his sight conspired against his peace; from overhead and all about came so audible and startling whispers and the sighs of creatures so obviously not of earth – that he could endure it no longer, and with a great effort to break some malign spell that bound his faculties to silence and inaction, he shouted with the full strength of his lungs! His voice, broken, it seemed, into an infinite multitude of unfamiliar sounds, went babbling and stammering away into the distant reaches of the forest, died into silence, and all was as before. But he had made a beginning at resistance and was encouraged.

He said: 'I will not submit unheard. There may be powers that are not malignant travelling this accursed road. I shall leave them a record and an appeal. I shall relate my wrongs, the persecutions that I endure – I, a helpless mortal, a penitent, an unoffending poet!' Halpin Frayser was a poet only as he was a penitent: in his dream.

Taking from his clothing a small red-leather pocket-book, one half of which was leaved for memoranda, he discovered that he was without a pencil. He broke a twig from a bush, dipped it into a pool of blood and wrote rapidly. He had hardly touched the paper with the point of his twig when a low, wild peal of laughter broke out at a measureless distance away, and growing ever louder, seemed approaching ever nearer; a soulless, heartless, and unjoyous laugh, like that of the loon, solitary by the lakeside at midnight; a laugh which culminated in an

unearthly shout close at hand, then died away by slow gradations, as if
the accursed being that uttered it had withdrawn over the verge of the
world whence it had come. But the man felt that this was not so – that
it was nearby and had not moved.

A strange sensation began slowly to take possession of his body and
his mind. He could not have said which, if any, of his senses was
affected; he felt it rather as a consciousness – a mysterious mental
assurance of some overpowering presence – some supernatural malevolence different in kind from the invisible existences that swarmed about
him, and superior to them in power. He knew that it had uttered that
hideous laugh. And now it seemed to be approaching him; from what
direction he did not know – dared not conjecture. All his former fears
were forgotten or merged in the gigantic terror that now held him in
thrall. Apart from that, he had but one thought: to complete his written
appeal to the benign powers who, traversing the haunted wood, might
sometime rescue him if he should be denied the blessing of annihila-
tion. He wrote with terrible rapidity, the twig in his fingers rilling
blood without renewal; but in the middle of a sentence his hands
denied their service to his will, his arms fell to his sides, the book to the
earth; and powerless to move or cry out, he found himself staring into
the sharply drawn face and blank, dead eyes of his own mother,
standing white and silent in the garments of the grave!

❧ TWO ☙

In his youth Halpin Frayser had lived with his parents in Nashville,
Tennessee. The Fraysers were well-to-do, having a good position in
such society as had survived the wreck wrought by civil war. Their
children had the social and educational opportunities of their time and
place, and had responded to good associations and instruction with
agreeable manners and cultivated minds. Halpin being the youngest
and not over robust was perhaps a trifle 'spoiled'. He had the double
disadvantage of a mother's assiduity and a father's neglect. Frayser *père*
was what no Southern man of means is not – a politician. His country,
or rather his section and State, made demands upon his time and
attention so exacting that to those of his family he was compelled to
turn an ear partly deafened by the thunder of the political captains and
the shouting, his own included.

Young Halpin was of a dreamy, indolent and rather romantic turn, somewhat more addicted to literature than law, the profession to which he was bred. Among those of his relations who professed the modern faith of heredity it was well understood that in him the character of the late Myron Bayne, a maternal great-grandfather, had revisited the glimpses of the moon – by which orb Bayne had in his lifetime been sufficiently affected to be a poet of no small Colonial distinction. If not specially observed, it was observable that while a Frayser who was not the proud possessor of a sumptuous copy of the ancestral 'poetical works' (printed at the family expense, and long ago withdrawn from an inhospitable market) was a rare Frayser indeed, there was an illogical indisposition to honour the great deceased in the person of his spiritual successor. Halpin was pretty generally deprecated as an intellectual black sheep who was likely at any moment to disgrace the flock by bleating in metre. The Tennessee Fraysers were a practical folk – not practical in the popular sense of devotion to sordid pursuits, but having a robust contempt for any qualities unfitting a man for the wholesome vocation of politics.

In justice to young Halpin it should be said that while in him were pretty faithfully reproduced most of the mental and moral characteristics ascribed by history and family tradition to the famous Colonial bard, his succession to the gift and faculty divine was purely inferential. Not only had he never been known to court the Muse, but in truth he could not have written correctly a line of verse to save himself from the Killer of the Wise. Still, there was no knowing when the dormant faculty might wake and smite the lyre.

In the meantime the young man was rather a loose fish, anyhow. Between him and his mother was the most perfect sympathy, for secretly the lady was herself a devout disciple of the late and great Myron Bayne, though with the tact so generally and justly admired in her sex (despite the hardy calumniators who insist that it is essentially the same thing as cunning) she had always taken care to conceal her weakness from all eyes but those of him who shared it. Their common guilt in respect of that was an added tie between them. If in Halpin's youth his mother had 'spoiled' him he had assuredly done his part toward being spoiled. As he grew to such manhood as is attainable by a Southerner who does not care which way elections go, the attachment between him and his beautiful mother – whom from early childhood he had called Katy – became yearly stronger and more tender. In these two romantic natures was manifest in a signal way that neglected phenomenon, the dominance of the sexual element in all the relations of life, strengthening, softening, and beautifying even those of consanguinity. The two were nearly inseparable, and by strangers observing their manners were not infrequently mistaken for lovers.

Entering his mother's boudoir one day Halpin Frayser kissed her upon the forehead, toyed for a moment with a lock of her dark hair which had escaped from its confining pins, and said, with an obvious effort at calmness:

'Would you greatly mind, Katy, if I were called away to California for a few weeks?'

It was hardly needful for Katy to answer with her lips a question to which her tell-tale cheeks had made instant reply. Evidently she would greatly mind; and the tears, too, sprang into her large brown eyes as corroborative testimony.

'Ah, my son,' she said, looking up into his face with infinite tenderness, 'I should have known that this was coming. Did I not lie awake a half of the night weeping because, during the other half, Grandfather Bayne had come to me in a dream, and standing by his portrait – young, too, and handsome as that – pointed to yours on the same wall? And when I looked it seemed that I could not see the features; you had been painted with a face cloth, such as we put upon the dead. Your father has laughed at me, but you and I, dear, know that such things are not for nothing. And I saw below the edge of the cloth the marks of hands on your throat – forgive me, but we have not been used to keep such things from each other. Perhaps you have another interpretation. Perhaps it does not mean that you will go to California. Or maybe you will take me with you?'

It must be confessed that this ingenious interpretation of the dream in the light of newly discovered evidence did not wholly commend itself to the son's more logical mind; he had, for the moment at least, a conviction that it foreshadowed a more simple and immediate, if less tragic, disaster than a visit to the Pacific Coast. It was Halpin Frayser's impression that he was to be garroted on his native heath.

'Are there not medicinal springs in California?' Mrs Frayser resumed before he had time to give her the true reading of the dream – 'places where one recovers from rheumatism and neuralgia? Look – my fingers feel so stiff; and I am almost sure they have been giving me great pain while I slept.'

She held out her hands for his inspection. What diagnosis of her case the young man may have thought it best to conceal with a smile the historian is unable to state, but for himself he feels bound to say that fingers looking less stiff, and showing fewer evidences of even insensible pain, have seldom been submitted for medical inspection by even the fairest patient desiring a prescription of unfamiliar scenes.

The outcome of it was that of these two odd persons having equally odd notions of duty, the one went to California, as the interest of his client required, and the other remained at home in compliance with a wish that her husband was scarcely conscious of entertaining.

While in San Francisco Halpin Frayser was walking one dark night along the water-front of the city, when, with a suddenness that surprised and disconcerted him, he became a sailor. He was in fact 'shanghaied' aboard a gallant, gallant ship, and sailed for a far countree. Nor did his misfortunes end with the voyage; for the ship was cast ashore on an island of the South Pacific, and it was six years afterward when the survivors were taken off by a venturesome trading schooner and brought back to San Francisco.

Though poor in purse, Frayser was no less proud in spirit than he had been in the years that seemed ages and ages ago. He would accept no assistance from strangers, and it was while living with a fellow survivor near the town of St Helena, awaiting news and remittances from home, that he had gone gunning and dreaming.

⤙ THREE ⤚

The apparition confronting the dreamer in the haunted wood – the thing so like, yet so unlike, his mother – was horrible! It stirred no love nor longing in his heart; it came unattended with pleasant memories of a golden past – inspired no sentiment of any kind; all the finer emotions were swallowed up in fear. He tried to turn and run from before it, but his legs were as lead; he was unable to lift his feet from the ground. His arms hung helpless at his sides; of his eyes only he retained control, and these he dared not remove from the lustreless orbs of the apparition, which he knew was not a soul without a body, but that most dreadful of all existences infesting that haunted wood – a body without a soul! In its blank stare was neither love, nor pity, nor intelligence – nothing to which to address an appeal for mercy. 'An appeal will not lie,' he thought, with an absurd reversion to professional slang, making the situation more horrible, as the fire of a cigar might light up a tomb.

For a time, which seemed so long that the world grew grey with age and sin, and the haunted forest, having fulfilled its purpose in this monstrous culmination of its terrors, vanished out of his consciousness with all its sights and sounds, the apparition stood within a pace, regarding him with the mindless malevolence of a wild brute; then thrust its hands forward and sprang upon him with appalling ferocity! The act released his physical energies without unfettering his will; his mind was still spellbound, but his powerful body and agile limbs, endowed with a blind, insensate life of their own, resisted stoutly and well. For an instant he seemed to see this unnatural contest between a dead intelligence and a breathing mechanism only as a spectator – such fancies are in dreams; then he regained his identity almost as if by a leap forward into his body, and the straining automaton had a directing will as alert and fierce as that of its hideous antagonist.

But what mortal can cope with a creature of his dream? The imagination creating the enemy is already vanquished; the combat's result is the combat's cause. Despite his struggles – despite his strength and activity, which seemed wasted in a void, he felt the cold fingers close upon his throat. Borne backward to the earth, he saw above him the dead and drawn face within a hand's-breadth of his own, and then all was black. A sound as of the beating of distant drums – a murmur of swarming voices, a sharp, far cry signing all to silence, and Halpin Frayser dreamed that he was dead.

❦ FOUR ❦

A warm, clear night had been followed by a morning of drenching fog. At about the middle of the afternoon of the preceding day a little whiff of light vapour – a mere thickening of the atmosphere, the ghost of a cloud – had been observed clinging to the western side of Mount St Helena, away up along the barren altitudes near the summit. It was so thin, so diaphanous, so like a fancy made visible, that one would have said: 'Look quickly! in a moment it will be gone.'

In a moment it was visibly larger and denser. While with one edge it clung to the mountain, with the other it reached farther and farther out into the air above the lower slopes. At the same time it extended itself to north and south, joining small patches of mist that appeared to come out of the mountainside on exactly the same level, with an intelligent design to be absorbed. And so it grew and grew until the summit was shut out of view from the valley, and over the valley itself was an ever-extending canopy, opaque and grey. At Calistoga, which lies near the head of the valley and the foot of the mountain, there were a starless night and a sunless morning. The fog, sinking into the valley, had reached southward, swallowing up ranch after ranch, until it had blotted out the town of St Helena, nine miles away. The dust in the road was laid; trees were adrip with moisture; birds sat silent in their coverts; the morning light was wan and ghastly, with neither colour nor fire.

Two men left the town of St Helena at the first glimmer of dawn, and walked along the road northward up the valley toward Calistoga. They carried guns on their shoulders, yet no one having knowledge of such matters could have mistaken them for hunters of bird or beast. They were a deputy sheriff from Napa and a detective from San Francisco – Holker and Jaralson, respectively. Their business was man-hunting.

'How far is it?' inquired Holker, as they strode along, their feet stirring white the dust beneath the damp surface of the road.

'The White Church? Only a half mile farther,' the other answered. 'By the way,' he added, 'it is neither white nor a church; it is an abandoned schoolhouse, grey with age and neglect. Religious services were once held in it – when it was white, and there is a graveyard that would delight a poet. Can you guess why I sent for you, and told you to come armed?'

'Oh, I never have bothered you about things of that kind. I've always found you communicative when the time came. But if I may hazard a guess, you want me to help you arrest one of the corpses in the graveyard.'

'You remember Branscom?' said Jaralson, treating his companion's wit with the inattention that it deserved.

'The chap who cut his wife's throat? I ought; I wasted a week's work on him and had my expenses for my trouble. There is a reward of five hundred dollars, but none of us ever got a sight of him. You don't mean to say – '

'Yes, I do. He has been under the noses of you fellows all the time. He comes by night to the old graveyard at the White Church.'

'The devil! That's where they buried his wife.'

'Well, you fellows might have had sense enough to suspect that he would return to her grave sometime?'

'The very last place that anyone would have expected him to return to.'

'But you had exhausted all the other places. Learning your failure at them, I "laid for him" there.'

'And you found him?'

'Damn it! he found *me*. The rascal got the drop on me – regularly held me up and made me travel. It's God's mercy that he didn't go through me. Oh, he's a good one, and I fancy the half of that reward is enough for me if you're needy.'

Holker laughed good-humouredly, and explained that his creditors were never more importunate.

'I wanted merely to show you the ground, and arrange a plan with you,' the detective explained. 'I thought it as well for us to be armed, even in daylight.'

'The man must be insane,' said the deputy sheriff. 'The reward is for his capture and conviction. If he's mad he won't be convicted.'

Mr Holker was so profoundly affected by that possible failure of justice that he involuntarily stopped in the middle of the road, then resumed his walk with abated zeal.

'Well, he looks it,' assented Jaralson. 'I'm bound to admit that a more unshaven, unshorn, unkempt, and uneverything wretch I never saw outside the ancient and honourable order of tramps. But I've gone in for him, and can't make up my mind to let go. There's glory in it for us, anyhow. Not another soul knows that he is this side of the Mountains of the Moon.'

'All right,' Holker said; 'we will go and view the ground,' and he added, in the words of a once favourite inscription for tombstones: ' "where you must shortly lie" – I mean if old Branscom ever gets tired of you and your impertinent intrusion. By the way, I heard the other day that "Branscom" was not his real name.'

'What is?'

'I can't recall it. I had lost all interest in the wretch, and it did not fix itself in my memory – something like Pardee. The woman whose throat he had the bad taste to cut was a widow when he met her. She had come to California to look up some relatives – there are persons who will do that sometimes. But you know all that.'

'Naturally.'

'But not knowing the right name, by what happy inspiration did you find the right grave? The man who told me what the name was said it had been cut on the headboard.'

'I don't know the right grave.' Jaralson was apparently a trifle reluctant to admit his ignorance of so important a point of his plan. 'I have been watching about the place generally. A part of our work this morning will be to identify that grave. Here is the White Church.'

For a long distance the road had been bordered by fields on both sides, but now on the left there was a forest of oaks, madroños, and gigantic spruces whose lower parts only could be seen, dim and ghostly in the fog. The undergrowth was, in places, thick, but nowhere impenetrable. For some moments Holker saw nothing of the building, but as they turned into the woods it revealed itself in faint grey outline through the fog, looking huge and far away. A few steps more, and it was within an arm's length, distinct, dark with moisture, and insignificant in size. It had the usual country-schoolhouse form – belonged to the packing-box order of architecture; had an underpinning of stones, a moss-grown roof, and blank window spaces, whence both glass and sash had long departed. It was ruined, but not a ruin – a typical Californian substitute for what are known to guide-bookers abroad as 'monuments of the past'. With scarcely a glance at this uninteresting structure Jaralson moved on into the dripping undergrowth beyond.

'I will show you where he held me up,' he said. 'This is the graveyard.'

Here and there among the bushes were small enclosures containing graves, sometimes no more than one. They were recognised as graves by the discoloured stones or rotting boards at head and foot, leaning at all angles, some prostrate; by the ruined picket fences surrounding them; or, infrequently, by the mound itself showing its gravel through the fallen leaves. In many instances nothing marked the spot where lay the vestiges of some poor mortal – who, leaving 'a large circle of sorrowing friends', had been left by them in turn – except a depression in the earth, more lasting than that in the spirits of the mourners. The paths, if any paths had been, were long obliterated; trees of a considerable size had been permitted to grow up from the graves and thrust aside with root or branch the enclosing fences. Over all was that air of abandonment and decay which seems nowhere so fit and significant as in a village of the forgotten dead.

As the two men, Jaralson leading, pushed their way through the growth of young trees, that enterprising man suddenly stopped and brought up his shotgun to the height of his breast, uttered a low note of warning, and stood motionless, his eyes fixed upon something ahead. As well as he could, obstructed by brush, his companion, though seeing nothing, imitated the posture and so stood, prepared for what might ensue. A moment later Jaralson moved cautiously forward, the other following.

Under the branches of an enormous spruce lay the dead body of a man. Standing silent above it they noted such particulars as first strike the attention – the face, the attitude, the clothing; whatever most promptly and plainly answers the unspoken question of a sympathetic curiosity.

The body lay upon its back, the legs wide apart. One arm was thrust upward, the other outward; but the latter was bent acutely, and the hand was near the throat. Both hands were tightly clenched. The whole attitude was that of desperate but ineffectual resistance to – what?

Nearby lay a shotgun and a game bag through the meshes of which was seen the plumage of shot birds. All about were evidences of a furious struggle; small sprouts of poison-oak were bent and denuded of leaf and bark; dead and rotting leaves had been pushed into heaps and ridges on both sides of the legs by the action of other feet than theirs; alongside the hips were unmistakable impressions of human knees.

The nature of the struggle was made clear by a glance at the dead man's throat and face. While breast and hands were white, those were purple – almost black. The shoulders lay upon a low mound, and the head was turned back at an angle otherwise impossible, the expanded eyes staring blankly backward in a direction opposite to that of the feet. From the froth filling the open mouth the tongue protruded, black and swollen. The throat showed horrible contusions; not mere finger-marks, but bruises and lacerations wrought by two strong hands that must have buried themselves in the yielding flesh, maintaining their terrible grasp until long after death. Breast, throat, face, were wet; the clothing was saturated; drops of water, condensed from the fog, studded the hair and moustache.

All this the two men observed without speaking – almost at a glance. Then Holker said: 'Poor devil! he had a rough deal.'

Jaralson was making a vigilant circumspection of the forest, his shotgun held in both hands and at full cock, his finger upon the trigger.

'The work of a maniac,' he said, without withdrawing his eyes from the enclosing wood. 'It was done by Branscom – Pardee.'

Something half hidden by the disturbed leaves on the earth caught Holker's attention. It was a red-leather pocket-book. He picked it up and opened it. It contained leaves of white paper for memoranda, and upon the first leaf was the name 'Halpin Frayser'. Written in red on several succeeding leaves – scrawled as if in haste and barely legible – were the following lines, which Holker read aloud, while his companion continued scanning the dim grey confines of their narrow world and hearing matter of apprehension in the drip of water from every burdened branch:

'Enthralled by some mysterious spell, I stood
In the lit gloom of an enchanted wood.
    The cypress there and myrtle twined their boughs,
Significant, in baleful brotherhood.

The brooding willow whispered to the yew;
Beneath, the deadly nightshade and the rue,
    With immortelles self-woven into strange
Funereal shapes, and horrid nettles grew.

No song of bird nor any drone of bees,
Nor light leaf lifted by the wholesome breeze:
    The air was stagnant all, and Silence was
A living thing that breathed among the trees.

Conspiring spirits whispered in the gloom,
Half-heard, the stilly secrets of the tomb.
    With blood the trees were all adrip; the leaves
Shone in the witch-light with a ruddy bloom.

I cried aloud! – the spell, unbroken still,
Rested upon my spirit and my will.
    Unsouled, unhearted, hopeless and forlorn,
I strove with monstrous presages of ill!

At last the viewless – '

Holker ceased reading; there was no more to read. The manuscript broke off in the middle of a line.

'That sounds like Bayne,' said Jaralson, who was something of a scholar in his way. He had abated his vigilance and stood looking down at the body.

'Who's Bayne?' Holker asked rather incuriously.

'Myron Bayne, a chap who flourished in the early years of the nation – more than a century ago. Wrote mighty dismal stuff; I have his collected works. That poem is not among them, but it must have been omitted by mistake.'

'It is cold,' said Holker; 'let us leave here; we must have up the coroner from Napa.'

Jaralson said nothing, but made a movement in compliance. Passing the end of the slight elevation of earth upon which the dead man's head and shoulders lay, his foot struck some hard substance under the rotting forest leaves, and he took the trouble to kick it into view. It was a fallen headboard, and painted on it were the hardly decipherable words, 'Catharine Larue'.

'Larue, Larue!' exclaimed Holker, with sudden animation. 'Why, that is the real name of Branscom – not Pardee. And – bless my soul! how it all comes to me – the murdered woman's name had been Frayser!'

'There is some rascally mystery here,' said Detective Jaralson. 'I hate anything of that kind.'

There came to them out of the fog – seemingly from a great distance – the sound of a laugh, a low, deliberate, soulless laugh which had no more of joy than that of a hyena night-prowling in the desert; a laugh that rose by slow gradation, louder and louder, clearer, more distinct and terrible, until it seemed barely outside the narrow circle of their vision; a laugh so unnatural, so unhuman, so devilish, that it filled those hardy man-hunters with a sense of dread unspeakable! They did not move their weapons nor think of them; the menace of that horrible sound was not of the kind to be met with arms. As it had grown out of silence, so now it died away; from a culminating shout which had seemed almost in their ears, it drew itself away into the distance, until its failing notes, joyless and mechanical to the last, sank to silence at a measureless remove.

The Secret of Macarger's Gulch

✤ ONE ✤

North-westwardly from Indian Hill, about nine miles as the crow flies,
is Macarger's Gulch. It is not much of a gulch – a mere depression
between two wooded ridges of inconsiderable height. From its mouth
up to its head – for gulches, like rivers, have an anatomy of their own –
the distance does not exceed two miles, and the width at bottom is at
only one place more than a dozen yards; for most of the distance on
either side of the little brook which drains it in winter, and goes dry in
the early spring, there is no level ground at all; the steep slopes of the
hills covered with an almost impenetrable growth of manzanita and
chemisal, are parted by nothing but the width of the watercourse. No
one but an occasional enterprising hunter of the vicinity ever goes into
Macarger's Gulch, and five miles away it is unknown, even by name.
Within that distance in any direction are far more conspicuous
topographical features without names, and one might try in vain to
ascertain by local inquiry the origin of the name of this one.

About midway between the head and the mouth of Macarger's
Gulch, the hill on the right as you ascend is cloven by another gulch, a
short dry one, and at the junction of the two is a level space of two or
three acres, and there a few years ago stood an old board house
containing one small room. How the component parts of the house,
few and simple as they were, had been assembled at that almost
inaccessible point is a problem in the solution of which there would be
greater satisfaction than advantage. Possibly the creek bed is a re-
formed road. It is certain that the gulch was at one time pretty
thoroughly prospected by miners, who must have had some means of
getting in with at least pack animals carrying tools and supplies; their
profits, apparently, were not such as would have justified any considerable outlay to connect Macarger's Gulch with any centre of civilisation

enjoying the distinction of a sawmill. The house, however, was there, most of it. It lacked a door and a window frame, and the chimney of mud and stones had fallen into an unlovely heap, overgrown with rank weeds. Such humble furniture as there may once have been and much of the lower weather-boarding, had served as fuel in the camp fires of hunters; as had also, probably, the kerbing of an old well, which at the time I write of existed in the form of a rather wide but not very deep depression nearby.

One afternoon in the summer of 1874, I passed up Macarger's Gulch from the narrow valley into which it opens, by following the dry bed of the brook. I was quail-shooting and had made a bag of about a dozen birds by the time I had reached the house described, of whose existence I was until then unaware. After rather carelessly inspecting the ruin I resumed my sport, and having fairly good success prolonged it until near sunset, when it occurred to me that I was a long way from any human habitation – too far to reach one by nightfall. But in my game bag was food, and the old house would afford shelter, if shelter were needed on a warm and dewless night in the foothills of the Sierra Nevada, where one may sleep in comfort on the pine needles, without covering. I am fond of solitude and love the night, so my resolution to 'camp out' was soon taken, and by the time that it was dark I had made my bed of boughs and grasses in a corner of the room and was roasting a quail at a fire that I had kindled on the hearth. The smoke escaped out of the ruined chimney, the light illuminated the room with a kindly glow, and as I ate my simple meal of plain bird and drank the remains of a bottle of red wine which had served me all the afternoon in place of the water, which the region did not supply, I experienced a sense of comfort which better fare and accommodations do not always give.

Nevertheless, there was something lacking. I had a sense of comfort, but not of security. I detected myself staring more frequently at the open doorway and blank window than I could find warrant for doing. Outside these apertures all was black, and I was unable to repress a certain feeling of apprehension as my fancy pictured the outer world and filled it with unfriendly entities, natural and supernatural – chief among which, in their respective classes, were the grizzly bear, which I knew was occasionally still seen in that region, and the ghost, which I had reason to think was not. Unfortunately, our feelings do not always respect the law of probabilities, and to me that evening, the possible and the impossible were equally disquieting.

Everyone who has had experience in the matter must have observed that one confronts the actual and imaginary perils of the night with far less apprehension in the open air than in a house with an open doorway. I felt this now as I lay on my leafy couch in a corner of the room next to the chimney and permitted my fire to die out. So strong became my sense of the presence of something malign and menacing in the place, that I found myself almost unable to withdraw my eyes from the opening, as in the deepening darkness it became more and more indistinct. And when the last little flame flickered and went out I grasped the shotgun which I had laid at my side and actually turned the muzzle in the direction of the now invisible entrance, my thumb on one of the hammers, ready to cock the piece, my breath suspended, my muscles rigid and tense. But later I laid down the weapon with a sense of shame and mortification. What did I fear, and why? – I, to whom the night had been

> a more familiar face
> Than that of man –

I, in whom that element of hereditary superstition from which none of us is altogether free had given to solitude and darkness and silence only a more alluring interest and charm! I was unable to comprehend my folly, and losing in the conjecture the thing conjectured of, I fell asleep. And then I dreamed.

I was in a great city in a foreign land – a city whose people were of my own race, with minor differences of speech and costume; yet precisely what these were I could not say; my sense of them was indistinct. The city was dominated by a great castle upon an overlooking height whose name I knew, but could not speak. I walked through many streets, some broad and straight with high, modern buildings, some narrow, gloomy, and tortuous, between the gables of quaint old houses whose overhanging storeys, elaborately ornamented with carvings in wood and stone, almost met above my head.

I sought someone whom I had never seen, yet knew that I should recognise when found. My quest was not aimless and fortuitous; it had a definite method. I turned from one street into another without hesitation and threaded a maze of intricate passages, devoid of the fear of losing my way.

Presently I stopped before a low door in a plain stone house which might have been the dwelling of an artisan of the better sort, and without announcing myself, entered. The room, rather sparely furnished, and lighted by a single window with small diamond-shaped panes, had but two occupants: a man and a woman. They took no notice of my intrusion, a circumstance which, in the manner of dreams, appeared entirely natural. They were not conversing; they sat apart, unoccupied and sullen.

The woman was young and rather stout, with fine large eyes and a certain grave beauty; my memory of her expression is exceedingly vivid, but in dreams one does not observe the details of faces. About her shoulders was a plaid shawl. The man was older, dark, with an evil face made more forbidding by a long scar extending from near the left temple diagonally downward into the black moustache; though in my dreams it seemed rather to haunt the face as a thing apart – I can express it no otherwise – than to belong to it. The moment that I found the man and woman I knew them to be husband and wife.

What followed, I remember indistinctly; all was confused and inconsistent – made so, I think, by gleams of consciousness. It was as if two pictures, the scene of my dream, and my actual surroundings, had been blended, one overlying the other, until the former, gradually fading, disappeared, and I was broad awake in the deserted cabin, entirely and tranquilly conscious of my situation.

My foolish fear was gone, and opening my eyes I saw that my fire, not altogether burned out, had revived by the falling of a stick and was again lighting the room. I had probably slept only a few minutes, but my commonplace dream had somehow so strongly impressed me that I was no longer drowsy; and after a little while I rose, pushed the embers of my fire together, and lighting my pipe proceeded in a rather ludicrously methodical way to meditate upon my vision.

It would have puzzled me then to say in what respect it was worth attention. In the first moment of serious thought that I gave to the matter I recognised the city of my dream as Edinburgh, where I had never been; so if the dream was a memory it was a memory of pictures and description. The recognition somehow deeply impressed me; it was as if something in my mind insisted rebelliously against will and reason on the importance of all this. And that faculty, whatever it was, asserted also a control of my speech. 'Surely,' I said aloud, quite involuntarily, 'the MacGregors must have come here from Edinburgh.'

At the moment, neither the substance of this remark nor the fact of my making it, surprised me in the least; it seemed entirely natural that I should know the name of my dreamfolk and something of their history. But the absurdity of it all soon dawned upon me: I laughed aloud, knocked the ashes from my pipe and again stretched myself upon my bed of boughs and grass, where I lay staring absently into my failing fire, with no further thought of either my dream or my surroundings.

Suddenly the single remaining flame crouched for a moment, then, springing upward, lifted itself clear of its embers and expired in air. The darkness was absolute.

At that instant – almost, it seemed, before the gleam of the blaze had faded from my eyes – there was a dull, dead sound, as of some heavy body falling upon the floor, which shook beneath me as I lay. I sprang to a sitting posture and groped at my side for my gun; my notion was that some wild beast had leaped in through the open window. While the flimsy structure was still shaking from the impact I heard the sound of blows, the scuffling of feet upon the floor, and then – it seemed to come from almost within reach of my hand, the sharp shrieking of a woman in mortal agony. So horrible a cry I had never heard nor conceived; it utterly unnerved me; I was conscious for a moment of nothing but my own terror! Fortunately my hand now found the weapon of which it was in search, and the familiar touch somewhat restored me. I leaped to my feet, straining my eyes to pierce the darkness. The violent sounds had ceased, but more terrible than these, I heard, at what seemed long intervals, the faint intermittent gasping of some living, dying thing!

As my eyes grew accustomed to the dim light of the coals in the fireplace, I saw first the shapes of the door and window looking blacker than the black of the walls. Next, the distinction between wall and floor became discernible, and at last I was sensible to the form and full expanse of the floor from end to end and side to side. Nothing was visible and the silence was unbroken.

With a hand that shook a little, the other still grasping my gun, I restored my fire and made a critical examination of the place. There was nowhere any sign that the cabin had been entered. My own tracks were visible in the dust covering the floor, but there were no others. I relit my pipe, provided fresh fuel by ripping a thin board or two from the inside of the house – I did not care to go into the darkness out of doors – and passed the rest of the night smoking and thinking, and feeding my fire; not for added years of life would I have permitted that little flame to expire again.

Some years afterward I met in Sacramento a man named Morgan, to whom I had a note of introduction from a friend in San Francisco. Dining with him one evening at his home I observed various 'trophies' upon the wall, indicating that he was fond of shooting. It turned out that he was, and in relating some of his feats he mentioned having been in the region of my adventure.

'Mr Morgan,' I asked abruptly, 'do you know a place up there called Macarger's Gulch?'

'I have good reason to,' he replied; 'it was I who gave to the newspapers, last year, the accounts of the finding of the skeleton there.'

I had not heard of it; the accounts had been published, it appeared, while I was absent in the East.

'By the way,' said Morgan, 'the name of the gulch is a corruption; it should have been called "MacGregor's". My dear,' he added, speaking to his wife, 'Mr Elderson has upset his wine.'

That was hardly accurate – I had simply dropped it, glass and all.

'There was an old shanty once in the gulch,' Morgan resumed when the ruin wrought by my awkwardness had been repaired, 'but just previously to my visit it had been blown down, or rather blown away, for its *débris* was scattered all about, the very floor being parted, plank from plank. Between two of the sleepers still in position I and my companion observed the remnant of a plaid shawl, and examining it found that it was wrapped about the shoulders of the body of a woman; of course but little remained besides the bones, partly covered with fragments of clothing, and brown dry skin. But we will spare Mrs Morgan,' he added with a smile. The lady had indeed exhibited signs of disgust rather than sympathy.

'It is necessary to say, however,' he went on, 'that the skull was fractured in several places, as by blows of some blunt instrument; and that instrument itself – a pick-handle, still stained with blood – lay under the boards nearby.'

Mr Morgan turned to his wife. 'Pardon me, my dear,' he said with affected solemnity, 'for mentioning these disagreeable particulars, the natural though regrettable incidents of a conjugal quarrel – resulting, doubtless, from the luckless wife's insubordination.'

'I ought to be able to overlook it,' the lady replied with composure; 'you have so many times asked me to in those very words.'

I thought he seemed rather glad to go on with his story.

'From these and other circumstances,' he said, 'the coroner's jury found that the deceased, Janet MacGregor, came to her death from blows inflicted by some person to the jury unknown; but it was added that the evidence pointed strongly to her husband, Thomas MacGregor, as the guilty person. But Thomas MacGregor has never been found nor heard of. It was learned that the couple came from Edinburgh, but not – my dear, do you not observe that Mr Elderson's bone-plate has water in it?'

I had deposited a chicken bone in my finger bowl.

'In a little cupboard I found a photograph of MacGregor, but it did not lead to his capture.'

'Will you let me see it?' I said.

The picture showed a dark man with an evil face made more forbidding by a long scar extending from near the temple diagonally downward into the black moustache.

'By the way, Mr Elderson,' said my affable host, 'may I know why you asked about "Macarger's Gulch"?'

'I lost a mule near there once,' I replied, 'and the mischance has – has quite – upset me.'

'My dear,' said Mr Morgan, with the mechanical intonation of an interpreter translating, 'the loss of Mr Elderson's mule has peppered his coffee.'

One Summer Night

The fact that Henry Armstrong was buried did not seem to him to prove that he was dead: he had always been a hard man to convince. That he really was buried, the testimony of his senses compelled him to admit. His posture – flat upon his back, with his hands crossed upon his stomach and tied with something that he easily broke without profitably altering the situation – the strict confinement of his entire person, the black darkness and profound silence, made a body of evidence impossible to controvert and he accepted it without cavil.

But dead – no; he was only very, very ill. He had, withal, the invalid's apathy and did not greatly concern himself about the uncommon fate that had been allotted to him. No philosopher was he – just a plain, commonplace person gifted, for the time being, with a pathological indifference: the organ that he feared consequences with was torpid. So, with no particular apprehension for his immediate future, he fell asleep and all was peace with Henry Armstrong.

But something was going on overhead. It was a dark summer night, shot through with infrequent shimmers of lightning silently firing a cloud lying low in the west and portending a storm. These brief, stammering illuminations brought out with ghastly distinctness the monuments and headstones of the cemetery and seemed to set them dancing. It was not a night in which any credible witness was likely to be straying about a cemetery, so the three men who were there, digging into the grave of Henry Armstrong, felt reasonably secure.

Two of them were young students from a medical college a few miles away; the third was a gigantic negro known as Jess. For many years Jess had been employed about the cemetery as a man-of-all-work and it was his favourite pleasantry that he knew 'every soul in the place'. From the nature of what he was now doing it was inferable that the place was not so populous as its register may have shown it to be.

Outside the wall, at the part of the grounds farthest from the public road, were a horse and a light wagon, waiting.

The work of excavation was not difficult: the earth with which the grave had been loosely filled a few hours before offered little resistance and was soon thrown out. Removal of the casket from its box was less easy, but it was taken out, for it was a perquisite of Jess, who carefully unscrewed the cover and laid it aside, exposing the body in black trousers and white shirt. At that instant the air sprang to flame, a cracking shock of thunder shook the stunned world and Henry Armstrong tranquilly sat up. With inarticulate cries the men fled in terror, each in a different direction. For nothing on earth could two of them have been persuaded to return. But Jess was of another breed.

In the grey of the morning the two students, pallid and haggard from anxiety and with the terror of their adventure still beating tumultuously in their blood, met at the medical college.

'You saw it?' cried one.

'God! yes – what are we to do?'

They went around to the rear of the building, where they saw a horse, attached to a light wagon, hitched to a gatepost near the door of the dissecting-room. Mechanically they entered the room. On a bench in the obscurity sat the negro Jess. He rose, grinning, all eyes and teeth.

'I'm waiting for my pay,' he said.

Stretched naked on a long table lay the body of Henry Armstrong, the head defiled with blood and clay from a blow with a spade.

The Moonlit Road

❧ ONE ❧

Statement of Joel Hetman Jr

I am the most unfortunate of men. Rich, respected, fairly well educated and of sound health – with many other advantages usually valued by those having them and coveted by those who have them not – I sometimes think that I should be less unhappy if they had been denied me, for then the contrast between my outer and my inner life would not be continually demanding a painful attention. In the stress of privation and the need of effort I might sometimes forget the sombre secret ever baffling the conjecture that it compels.

I am the only child of Joel and Julia Hetman. The one was a well-to-do country gentleman, the other a beautiful and accomplished woman to whom he was passionately attached with what I now know to have been a jealous and exacting devotion. The family home was a few miles from Nashville, Tennessee, a large, irregularly built dwelling of no particular order of architecture, a little way off the road, in a park of trees and shrubbery.

At the time of which I write I was nineteen years old, a student at Yale. One day I received a telegram from my father of such urgency that in compliance with its unexplained demand I left at once for home. At the railway station in Nashville a distant relative awaited me to apprise me of the reason for my recall: my mother had been barbarously murdered – why and by whom none could conjecture, but the circumstances were these:

My father had gone to Nashville, intending to return the next afternoon. Something prevented his accomplishing the business in hand, so he returned on the same night, arriving just before the dawn. In his testimony before the coroner he explained that having no latchkey and not caring to disturb the sleeping servants, he had, with no clearly defined intention, gone round to the rear of the house. As he turned an angle of the building, he heard a sound as of a door gently closed, and saw in the darkness, indistinctly, the figure of a man, which instantly disappeared among the trees of the lawn. A hasty pursuit and brief search of the grounds in the belief that the trespasser was someone secretly visiting a servant proving fruitless, he entered at the unlocked door and mounted the stairs to my mother's chamber. Its door was open, and stepping into black darkness he fell headlong over some heavy object on the floor. I may spare myself the details; it was my poor mother, dead of strangulation by human hands!

Nothing had been taken from the house, the servants had heard no sound, and excepting those terrible fingermarks upon the dead woman's throat – dear God! that I might forget them! – no trace of the assassin was ever found.

I gave up my studies and remained with my father, who, naturally, was greatly changed. Always of a sedate, taciturn disposition, he now fell into so deep a dejection that nothing could hold his attention, yet anything – a footfall, the sudden closing of a door – aroused in him a fitful interest; one might have called it an apprehension. At any small surprise of the senses he would start visibly and sometimes turn pale, then relapse into a melancholy apathy deeper than before. I suppose he was what is called a 'nervous wreck'. As to me, I was younger then than now – there is much in that. Youth is Gilead, in which is balm for every wound. Ah, that I might again dwell in that enchanted land! Unacquainted with grief, I knew not how to appraise my bereavement; I could not rightly estimate the strength of the stroke.

One night, a few months after the dreadful event, my father and I walked home from the city. The full moon was about three hours above the eastern horizon; the entire countryside had the solemn stillness of a summer night; our footfalls and the ceaseless song of the katydids were the only sound, aloof. Black shadows of bordering trees lay athwart the road, which, in the short reaches between, gleamed a ghostly white. As we approached the gate to our dwelling, whose front was in shadow, and in which no light shone, my father suddenly stopped and clutched my arm, saying, hardly above his breath: 'God! God! what is that?'

'I hear nothing,' I replied.

'But see – see!' he said, pointing along the road, directly ahead.

I said: 'Nothing is there. Come, father, let us go in – you are ill.'

He had released my arm and was standing rigid and motionless in the centre of the illuminated roadway, staring like one bereft of sense. His face in the moonlight showed a pallor and fixity inexpressibly distressing. I pulled gently at his sleeve, but he had forgotten my existence. Presently he began to retire backward, step by step, never for an instant removing his eyes from what he saw, or thought he saw. I turned half round to follow, but stood irresolute. I do not recall any feeling of fear, unless a sudden chill was its physical manifestation. It seemed as if an icy wind had touched my face and enfolded my body from head to foot; I could feel the stir of it in my hair.

At that moment my attention was drawn to a light that suddenly streamed from an upper window of the house: one of the servants, awakened by what mysterious premonition of evil who can say, and in obedience to an impulse that she was never able to name, had lit a lamp. When I turned to look for my father he was gone, and in all the years that have passed no whisper of his fate has come across the borderland of conjecture from the realm of the unknown.

⋙ TWO ⋘

Statement of Caspar Grattan

Today I am said to live; tomorrow, here in this room, will lie a senseless shape of clay that all too long was I. If anyone lift the cloth from the face of that unpleasant thing it will be in gratification of a mere morbid curiosity. Some, doubtless, will go further and inquire, 'Who was he?' In this writing I supply the only answer that I am able to make – Caspar Grattan. Surely, that should be enough. The name has served my small need for more than twenty years of a life of unknown length. True, I gave it to myself, but lacking another I had the right. In this world one must have a name; it prevents confusion, even when it does not establish identity. Some, though, are known by numbers, which also seem inadequate distinctions.

One day, for illustration, I was passing along a street of a city, far from here, when I met two men in uniform, one of whom, half pausing and looking curiously into my face, said to his companion, 'That man looks like 767.' Something in the number seemed familiar and horrible. Moved by an uncontrollable impulse, I sprang into a side street and ran until I fell exhausted in a country lane.

I have never forgotten that number, and always it comes to memory attended by gibbering obscenity, peals of joyless laughter, the clang of iron doors. So I say a name, even if self-bestowed, is better than a number. In the register of the potter's field I shall soon have both. What wealth!

Of him who shall find this paper I must beg a little consideration. It is not the history of my life; the knowledge to write that is denied me. This is only a record of broken and apparently unrelated memories, some of them as distinct and sequent as brilliant beads upon a thread, others remote and strange, having the character of crimson dreams with interspaces blank and black – witch-fires glowing still and red in a great desolation.

Standing upon the shore of eternity, I turn for a last look landward over the course by which I came. There are twenty years of footprints fairly distinct, the impressions of bleeding feet. They lead through poverty and pain, devious and unsure, as of one staggering beneath a burden –

Remote, unfriended, melancholy, slow.

Ah, the poet's prophecy of Me – how admirable, how dreadfully admirable!

Backward beyond the beginning of this *via dolorosa* – this epic of suffering with episodes of sin – I see nothing clearly; it comes out of a cloud. I know that it spans only twenty years, yet I am an old man.

One does not remember one's birth – one has to be told. But with me it was different; life came to me full-handed and dowered me with all my faculties and powers. Of a previous existence I know no more than others, for all have stammering intimations that may be memories and may be dreams. I know only that my first consciousness was of maturity in body and mind – a consciousness accepted without surprise or conjecture. I merely found myself walking in a forest, half-clad, footsore, unutterably weary and hungry. Seeing a farmhouse, I approached and asked for food, which was given me by one who inquired my name. I did not know, yet knew that all had names. Greatly embarrassed, I retreated, and night coming on, lay down in the forest and slept.

The next day I entered a large town which I shall not name. Nor shall I recount further incidents of the life that is now to end – a life of wandering, always and everywhere haunted by an overmastering sense of crime in punishment of wrong and of terror in punishment of crime. Let me see if I can reduce it to narrative.

I seem once to have lived near a great city, a prosperous planter, married to a woman whom I loved and distrusted. We had, it sometimes seems, one child, a youth of brilliant parts and promise. He is at all times a vague figure, never clearly drawn, frequently altogether out of the picture.

One luckless evening it occurred to me to test my wife's fidelity in a vulgar, commonplace way familiar to everyone who has acquaintance with the literature of fact and fiction. I went to the city, telling my wife that I should be absent until the following afternoon. But I returned before daybreak and went to the rear of the house, purposing to enter by a door with which I had secretly so tampered that it would seem to lock, yet not actually fasten. As I approached it, I heard it gently open and close, and saw a man steal away into the darkness. With murder in my heart, I sprang after him, but he had vanished without even the bad luck of identification. Sometimes now I cannot even persuade myself that it was a human being.

Crazed with jealousy and rage, blind and bestial with all the elemental passions of insulted manhood, I entered the house and sprang up the stairs to the door of my wife's chamber. It was closed, but having tampered with its lock also, I easily entered, and despite the black darkness soon stood by the side of her bed. My groping hands told me that although disarranged it was unoccupied.

'She is below,' I thought, 'and terrified by my entrance has evaded me in the darkness of the hall.'

With the purpose of seeking her I turned to leave the room, but took a wrong direction – the right one! My foot struck her, cowering in a corner of the room. Instantly my hands were at her throat, stifling a shriek, my knees were upon her struggling body; and there in the darkness, without a word of accusation or reproach, I strangled her till she died!

There ends the dream. I have related it in the past tense, but the present would be the fitter form, for again and again the sombre tragedy re-enacts itself in my consciousness – over and over I lay the plan, I suffer the confirmation, I redress the wrong. Then all is blank; and afterward the rains beat against the grimy window-panes, or the snows fall upon my scant attire, the wheels rattle in the squalid streets where my life lies in poverty and mean employment. If there is ever sunshine I do not recall it; if there are birds they do not sing.

There is another dream, another vision of the night. I stand among the shadows in a moonlit road. I am aware of another presence, but whose I cannot rightly determine. In the shadow of a great dwelling I catch the gleam of white garments; then the figure of a woman confronts me in the road – my murdered wife! There is death in the face; there are marks upon the throat. The eyes are fixed on mine with an infinite gravity which is not reproach, nor hate, nor menace, nor anything less terrible than recognition. Before this awful apparition I retreat in terror – a terror that is upon me as I write. I can no longer rightly shape the words. See! they –

Now I am calm, but truly there is no more to tell: the incident ends where it began – in darkness and in doubt.

Yes, I am again in control of myself: 'the captain of my soul.' But that is not respite; it is another stage and phase of expiation. My penance, constant in degree, is mutable in kind: one of its variants is tranquillity. After all, it is only a life-sentence. 'To Hell for life' – that is a foolish penalty: the culprit chooses the duration of his punishment. Today my term expires.

To each and all, the peace that was not mine.

᧧ THREE ᧨

Statement of the late Julia Hetman,
through the medium Bayrolles

I had retired early and fallen almost immediately into a peaceful sleep, from which I awoke with that indefinable sense of peril which is, I think, a common experience in that other, earlier life. Of its unmeaning character, too, I was entirely persuaded, yet that did not banish it. My husband, Joel Hetman, was away from home; the servants slept in another part of the house. But these were familiar conditions; they had never before distressed me. Nevertheless, the strange terror grew so insupportable that conquering my reluctance to move I sat up and lit the lamp at my bedside. Contrary to my expectation this gave me no relief; the light seemed rather an added danger, for I reflected that it would shine out under the door, disclosing my presence to whatever evil thing might lurk outside. You that are still in the flesh, subject to horrors of the imagination, think what a monstrous fear that must be which seeks in darkness security from malevolent existences of the night. That is to spring to close quarters with an unseen enemy – the strategy of despair!

Extinguishing the lamp I pulled the bedclothing about my head and lay trembling and silent, unable to shriek, forgetful to pray. In this pitiable state I must have lain for what you call hours – with us there are no hours, there is no time.

At last it came – a soft, irregular sound of footfalls on the stairs! They were slow, hesitant, uncertain, as of something that did not see its way; to my disordered reason all the more terrifying for that, as the approach of some blind and mindless malevolence to which is no appeal. I even thought that I must have left the hall lamp burning and the groping of this creature proved it a monster of the night. This was foolish and inconsistent with my previous dread of the light, but what would you have? Fear has no brains; it is an idiot. The dismal witness that it bears and the cowardly counsel that it whispers are unrelated. We know this well, we who have passed into the Realm of Terror, who skulk in eternal dusk among the scenes of our former lives, invisible even to ourselves, and one another, yet hiding forlorn in lonely places; yearning for speech with our loved ones, yet dumb, and as fearful of them as they of us. Sometimes the disability is removed, the law suspended: by the deathless power of love or hate we break the spell – we are seen by those whom we would warn, console, or punish. What form we seem to them to bear we know not; we know only that we terrify even those whom we most wish to comfort, and from whom we most crave tenderness and sympathy.

Forgive, I pray you, this inconsequent digression by what was once a woman. You who consult us in this imperfect way – you do not understand. You ask foolish questions about things unknown and things forbidden. Much that we know and could impart in our speech is meaningless in yours. We must communicate with you through a stammering intelligence in that small fraction of our language that you yourselves can speak. You think that we are of another world. No, we have knowledge of no world but yours, though for us it holds no sunlight, no warmth, no music, no laughter, no song of birds, nor any companionship. O God! what a thing it is to be a ghost, cowering and shivering in an altered world, a prey to apprehension and despair!

No, I did not die of fright: the Thing turned and went away. I heard it go down the stairs, hurriedly, I thought, as if itself in sudden fear. Then I rose to call for help. Hardly had my shaking hand found the doorknob when – merciful heaven! – I heard it returning. Its footfalls as it remounted the stairs were rapid, heavy and loud; they shook the house. I fled to an angle of the wall and crouched upon the floor. I tried to pray. I tried to call the name of my dear husband. Then I heard the door thrown open. There was an interval of unconsciousness, and when I revived I felt a strangling clutch upon my throat – felt my arms feebly beating against something that bore me backward – felt my tongue thrusting itself from between my teeth! And then I passed into this life.

No, I have no knowledge of what it was. The sum of what we knew at death is the measure of what we know afterward of all that went before. Of this existence we know many things, but no new light falls upon any page of that; in memory is written all of it that we can read. Here are no heights of truth overlooking the confused landscape of that dubitable domain. We still dwell in the Valley of the Shadow, lurk in its desolate places, peering from brambles and thickets at its mad, malign inhabitants. How should we have new knowledge of that fading past?

What I am about to relate happened on a night. We know when it is night, for then you retire to your houses and we can venture from our places of concealment to move unafraid about our old homes, to look in at the windows, even to enter and gaze upon your faces as you sleep. I had lingered long near the dwelling where I had been so cruelly changed to what I am, as we do while any that we love or hate remain. Vainly I had sought some method of manifestation, some way to make my continued existence and my great love and poignant pity under-stood by my husband and son. Always if they slept they would wake, or if in my desperation I dared approach them when they were awake, would turn toward me the terrible eyes of the living, frightening me by the glances that I sought from the purpose that I held.

On this night I had searched for them without success, fearing to find them; they were nowhere in the house, nor about the moonlit dawn. For, although the sun is lost to us for ever, the moon, full-orbed or slender, remains to us. Sometimes it shines by night, sometimes by day, but always it rises and sets, as in that other life.

I left the lawn and moved in the white light and silence along the road, aimless and sorrowing. Suddenly I heard the voice of my poor husband in exclamations of astonishment, with that of my son in reassurance and dissuasion; and there by the shadow of a group of trees they stood – near, so near! Their faces were toward me, the eyes of the elder man fixed upon mine. He saw me – at last, at last, he saw me! In the consciousness of that, my terror fled as a cruel dream. The death-spell was broken: Love had conquered Law! Mad with exultation I shouted – I *must* have shouted, 'He sees, he sees: he will understand!' Then, controlling myself, I moved forward, smiling and consciously beautiful, to offer myself to his arms, to comfort him with endearments, and, with my son's hand in mine, to speak words that should restore the broken bonds between the living and the dead.

Alas! alas! his face went white with fear, his eyes were as those of a hunted animal. He backed away from me, as I advanced, and at last turned and fled into the wood – whither, it is not given to me to know.

To my poor boy, left doubly desolate, I have never been able to impart a sense of my presence. Soon he, too, must pass to this Life Invisible and be lost to me for ever.

A Diagnosis of Death

'I am not so superstitious as some of your physicians – men of science, as you are pleased to be called,' said Hawver, replying to an accusation that had not been made. 'Some of you – only a few, I confess – believe in the immortality of the soul, and in apparitions which you have not the honesty to call ghosts. I go no further than a conviction that the living are sometimes seen where they are not, but have been – where they have lived so long, perhaps so intensely, as to have left their impress on everything about them. I know, indeed, that one's environment may be so affected by one's personality as to yield, long afterward, an image of one's self to the eyes of another. Doubtless the impressing personality has to be the right kind of personality as the perceiving eyes have to be the right kind of eyes – mine, for example.'

'Yes, the right kind of eyes, conveying sensations to the wrong kind of brain,' said Dr Frayley, smiling.

'Thank you; one likes to have an expectation gratified; that is about the reply that I supposed you would have the civility to make.'

'Pardon me. But you say that you know. That is a good deal to say, don't you think? Perhaps you will not mind the trouble of saying how you learned.'

'You will call it an hallucination,' Hawver said, 'but that does not matter.' And he told the story.

'Last summer I went, as you know, to pass the hot weather term in the town of Meridian. The relative at whose house I had intended to stay was ill, so I sought other quarters. After some difficulty I succeeded in renting a vacant dwelling that had been occupied by an eccentric doctor of the name of Mannering, who had gone away years before, no one knew where, not even his agent. He had built the house himself and had lived in it with an old servant for about ten years. His practice, never very extensive, had after a few years been given up entirely. Not only so, but he had withdrawn himself almost altogether from social life and become a recluse. I was told by the village doctor, about the only person with whom he held any relations, that during his retirement he had devoted himself to a single line of study, the result of which he had expounded in a book that did not commend itself to the approval of his professional brethren, who, indeed, considered him not entirely sane. I have not seen the book and cannot now recall the title of it, but I am told that it expounded a rather startling theory. He held that it was possible in the case of many a person in good health to forecast his death with precision, several months in advance of the event. The limit, I think, was eighteen months. There were local tales of his having exerted his powers of prognosis, or perhaps you would say diagnosis; and it was said that in every instance the person whose friends he had warned had died suddenly at the appointed time, and from no assignable cause. All this, however, has nothing to do with what I have to tell; I thought it might amuse a physician.

'The house was furnished, just as he had lived in it. It was a rather gloomy dwelling for one who was neither a recluse nor a student, and I think it gave something of its character to me – perhaps some of its former occupant's character; for always I felt in it a certain melancholy that was not in my natural disposition, nor, I think, due to loneliness. I had no servants that slept in the house, but I have always been, as you know, rather fond of my own society, being much addicted to reading, though little to study. Whatever was the cause, the effect was dejection and a sense of impending evil; this was especially so in Dr Mannering's study, although that room was the lightest and most airy in the house. The doctor's life-size portrait in oil hung in that room, and seemed completely to dominate it. There was nothing unusual in the picture; the man was evidently rather good-looking, about fifty years old, with iron-grey hair, a smooth-shaven face and dark, serious eyes. Something in the picture always drew and held my attention. The man's appearance became familiar to me, and rather "haunted" me.

'One evening I was passing through this room to my bedroom, with a lamp – there is no gas in Meridian. I stopped as usual before the portrait, which seemed in the lamplight to have a new expression, not easily named, but distinctly uncanny. It interested but did not disturb me. I moved the lamp from one side to the other and observed the effects of the altered light. While so engaged I felt an impulse to turn round. As I did so I saw a man moving across the room directly toward me! As soon as he came near enough for the lamplight to illuminate the face I saw that it was Dr Mannering himself; it was as if the portrait were walking!

' "I beg your pardon," I said, somewhat coldly, "but if you knocked I did not hear."

'He passed me, within an arm's length, lifted his right forefinger, as in warning, and without a word went on out of the room, though I observed his exit no more than I had observed his entrance.

'Of course, I need not tell you that this was what you will call a hallucination and I call an apparition. That room had only two doors, of which one was locked; the other led into a bedroom, from which there was no exit. My feeling on realising this is not an important part of the incident.

'Doubtless this seems to you a very commonplace "ghost story" – one constructed on the regular lines laid down by the old masters of the art. If that were so I should not have related it, even if it were true. The man was not dead; I met him today in Union Street. He passed me in a crowd.'

Hawver had finished his story and both men were silent. Dr Frayley absently drummed on the table with his fingers.

'Did he say anything today?' he asked – 'anything from which you inferred that he was not dead?'

Hawver stared and did not reply.

'Perhaps,' continued Frayley, 'he made a sign, a gesture – lifted a finger, as in warning. It's a trick he had – a habit when saying something serious – announcing the result of a diagnosis, for example.'

'Yes, he did – just as his apparition had done. But, good God! did you ever know him?'

Hawver was apparently growing nervous.

'I knew him. I have read his book, as will every physician someday. It is one of the most striking and important of the century's contributions to medical science. Yes, I knew him; I attended him in an illness three years ago. He died.'

Hawver sprang from his chair, manifestly disturbed. He strode forward and back across the room; then approached his friend, and in a voice not altogether steady, said: 'Doctor, have you anything to say to me as a physician?'

'No, Hawver; you are the healthiest man I ever knew. As a friend I advise you to go to your room. You play the violin like an angel. Play it; play something light and lively. Get this cursed bad business off your mind.'

The next day Hawver was found dead in his room, the violin at his neck, the bow upon the string, his music open before him at Chopin's Funeral March.

Moxon's Master

'Are you serious? – do you really believe that a machine thinks?'

I got no immediate reply; Moxon was apparently intent upon the coals in the grate, touching them deftly here and there with the fire-poker till they signified a sense of his attention by a brighter glow. For several weeks I had been observing in him a growing habit of delay in answering even the most trivial of commonplace questions. His air, however, was that of preoccupation rather than deliberation: one might have said that he had 'something on his mind'.

Presently he said:

'What is a "machine"? The word has been variously defined. Here is one definition from a popular dictionary: "Any instrument or organisation by which power is applied and made effective, or a desired effect produced." Well, then, is not a man a machine? And you will admit that he thinks – or thinks he thinks.'

'If you do not wish to answer my question,' I said, rather testily, 'why not say so? – all that you say is mere evasion. You know well enough that when I say "machine" I do not mean a man, but something that man has made and controls.'

'When it does not control him,' he said, rising abruptly and looking out of a window, whence nothing was visible in the blackness of a stormy night. A moment later he turned about and with a smile said: 'I beg your pardon; I had no thought of evasion. I considered the dictionary man's unconscious testimony suggestive and worth some-thing in the discussion. I can give your question a direct answer easily enough: I do believe that a machine thinks about the work that it is doing.'

That was direct enough, certainly. It was not altogether pleasing, for it tended to confirm a sad suspicion that Moxon's devotion to study and work in his machine-shop had not been good for him. I knew, for one thing, that he suffered from insomnia, and that is no light affliction. Had it affected his mind? His reply to my question seemed to me then evidence that it had; perhaps I should think differently about it now. I was younger then, and among the blessings that are not denied to youth is ignorance. Incited by that great stimulant to controversy, I said: 'And what, pray, does it think with – in the absence of a brain?'

The reply, coming with less than his customary delay, took his favourite form of counter-interrogation: 'With what does a plant think – in the absence of a brain?'

'Ah, plants also belong to the philosopher class! I should be pleased to know some of their conclusions; you may omit the premises.'

'Perhaps,' he replied, apparently unaffected by my foolish irony, 'you may be able to infer their convictions from their acts. I will spare you the familiar examples of the sensitive mimosa, the several insectivorous flowers and those whose stamens bend down and shake their pollen upon the entering bee in order that he may fertilise their distant mates. But observe this. In an open spot in my garden I planted a climbing vine. When it was barely above the surface I set a stake into the soil a yard away. The vine at once made for it, but as it was about to reach it after several days I removed it a few feet. The vine at once altered its course, making an acute angle, and again made for the stake. This manœuvre was repeated several times, but finally, as if discouraged, the vine abandoned the pursuit and ignoring further attempts to divert it, travelled to a small tree, farther away, which it climbed.

'Roots of the eucalyptus will prolong themselves incredibly in search of moisture. A well-known horticulturist relates that one entered an old drain pipe and followed it until it came to a break, where a section of the pipe had been removed to make way for a stone wall that had been built across its course. The root left the drain and followed the wall until it found an opening where a stone had fallen out. It crept through and following the other side of the wall back to the drain, entered the unexplored part and resumed its journey.'

'And all this?'

'Can you miss the significance of it? It shows the consciousness of plants. It proves that they think.'

'Even if it did – what then? We were speaking, not of plants, but of machines. They may be composed partly of wood – wood that has no longer vitality – or wholly of metal. Is thought an attribute also of the mineral kingdom?'

'How else do you explain the phenomena, for example, of crystallisation?'

'I do not explain them.'

'Because you cannot without affirming what you wish to deny, namely, intelligent co-operation among the constituent elements of the crystals. When soldiers form lines, or hollow squares, you call it reason. When wild geese in flight take the form of a letter V you say instinct. When the homogeneous atoms of a mineral, moving freely in solution, arrange themselves into shapes mathematically perfect, or particles of frozen moisture into the symmetrical and beautiful forms of snowflakes, you have nothing to say. You have not even invented a name to conceal your heroic unreason.'

Moxon was speaking with unusual animation and earnestness. As he paused I heard in an adjoining room known to me as his 'machine-shop', which no one but himself was permitted to enter, a singular thumping sound, as of someone pounding upon a table with an open hand. Moxon heard it at the same moment and, visibly agitated, rose and hurriedly passed into the room whence it came. I thought it odd that anyone else should be in there, and my interest in my friend – with doubtless a touch of unwarrantable curiosity – led me to listen intently, though, I am happy to say, not at the keyhole. There were confused sounds, as of a struggle or scuffle; the floor shook. I distinctly heard hard breathing and a hoarse whisper which said 'Damn you!' Then all was silent, and presently Moxon reappeared and said, with a rather sorry smile:

'Pardon me for leaving you so abruptly. I have a machine in there that lost its temper and cut up rough.'

Fixing my eyes steadily upon his left cheek, which was traversed by four parallel excoriations showing blood, I said: 'How would it do to trim its nails?'

I could have spared myself the jest; he gave it no attention, but seated himself in the chair that he had left and resumed the interrupted monologue as if nothing had occurred:

'Doubtless you do not hold with those (I need not name them to a man of your reading) who have taught that all matter is sentient, that every atom is a living, feeling, conscious being. *I* do. There is no such thing as dead, inert matter: it is all alive; all instinct with force, actual and potential; all sensitive to the same forces in its environment and susceptible to the contagion of higher and subtler ones residing in such superior organisms as it may be brought into relation with, as those of man when he is fashioning it into an instrument of his will. It absorbs something of his intelligence and purpose – more of them in proportion to the complexity of the resulting machine and that of its work.

'Do you happen to recall Herbert Spencer's definition of "Life"? I read it thirty years ago. He may have altered it afterward, for anything I know, but in all that time I have been unable to think of a single word that could profitably be changed or added or removed. It seems to me not only the best definition, but the only possible one.

' "Life," he says, "is a definite combination of heterogeneous changes, both simultaneous and successive, in correspondence with external coexistences and sequences." '

'That defines the phenomenon,' I said, 'but gives no hint of its cause.'

'That,' he replied, 'is all that any definition can do. As Mill points out, we know nothing of cause except as an antecedent – nothing of effect except as a consequent. Of certain phenomena, one never occurs without another, which is dissimilar: the first in point of time we call cause, the second, effect. One who had many times seen a rabbit pursued by a dog, and had never seen rabbits and dogs otherwise, would think the rabbit the cause of the dog.

'But I fear,' he added, laughing naturally enough, 'that my rabbit is leading me a long way from the track of my legitimate quarry: I'm indulging in the pleasure of the chase for its own sake. What I want you to observe is that in Herbert Spencer's definition of "Life" the activity of a machine is included – there is nothing in the definition that is not applicable to it. According to this sharpest of observers and deepest of thinkers, if a man during his period of activity is alive, so is a machine when in operation. As an inventor and constructor of machines I know that to be true.'

Moxon was silent for a long time, gazing absently into the fire. It was growing late and I thought it time to be going, but somehow I did not like the notion of leaving him in that isolated house, all alone except for the presence of some person of whose nature my conjectures could go no further than that it was unfriendly, perhaps malign. Leaning toward him and looking earnestly into his eyes while making a motion with my hand through the door of his workshop, I said: 'Moxon, whom have you in there?'

Somewhat to my surprise he laughed lightly and answered without hesitation: 'Nobody; the incident that you have in mind was caused by my folly in leaving a machine in action with nothing to act upon, while I undertook the interminable task of enlightening your understanding. Do you happen to know that Consciousness is the creature of Rhythm?'

'O bother them both!' I replied, rising and laying hold of my overcoat. 'I'm going to wish you good-night; and I'll add the hope that the machine which you inadvertently left in action will have her gloves on the next time you think it needful to stop her.'

Without waiting to observe the effect of my shot I left the house.

Rain was falling, and the darkness was intense. In the sky beyond the crest of a hill toward which I groped my way along precarious plank sidewalks and across miry, unpaved streets I could see the faint glow of the city's lights, but behind me nothing was visible but a single window of Moxon's house. It glowed with what seemed to me a mysterious and fateful meaning. I knew it was an uncurtained aperture in my friend's 'machine-shop', and I had little doubt that he had resumed the studies interrupted by his duties as my instructor in mechanical consciousness and the fatherhood of Rhythm. Odd, and in some degree humorous, as his convictions seemed to me at that time, I could not wholly divest myself of the feeling that they had some tragic relation to his life and character – perhaps to his destiny – although I no longer entertained the notion that they were the vagaries of a disordered mind. Whatever might be thought of his views, his exposition of them was too logical for that. Over and over, his last words came back to me: 'Consciousness is the creature of Rhythm.' Bald and terse as the statement was, I now found it infinitely alluring. At each recurrence it broadened in meaning and deepened in suggestion. Why, here (I thought) is something upon which to found a philosophy. If Consciousness is the product of Rhythm all things *are* conscious, for all have motion, and all motion is rhythmic. I wondered if Moxon knew the significance and breadth of his thought – the scope of this momentous generalisation; or had he arrived at his philosophic faith by the tortuous and uncertain road of observation?

That faith was then new to me, and all Moxon's expounding had failed to make me a convert; but now it seemed as if a great light shone about me, like that which fell upon Saul of Tarsus; and out there in the storm and darkness and solitude I experienced what Lewes calls 'the endless variety and excitement of philosophic thought'. I exulted in a new sense of knowledge, a new pride of reason. My feet seemed hardly to touch the earth; it was as if I were uplifted and borne through the air by invisible wings.

Yielding to an impulse to seek further light from him whom I now recognised as my master and guide, I had unconsciously turned about, and almost before I was aware of having done so found myself again at Moxon's door. I was drenched with rain, but felt no discomfort. Unable in my excitement to find the doorbell I instinctively tried the knob. It turned and, entering, I mounted the stairs to the room that I had so recently left. All was dark and silent; Moxon, as I had supposed, was in the adjoining room – the 'machine-shop'. Groping along the wall until I found the communicating door I knocked loudly several times, but got no response, which I attributed to the uproar outside, for the wind was blowing a gale and dashing the rain against the thin walls in sheets. The drumming upon the shingle roof spanning the unceilinged room was loud and incessant.

I had never been invited into the machine-shop – had, indeed, been denied admittance, as had all others, with one exception, a skilled metal worker, of whom no one knew anything except that his name was Haley and his habit silence. But in my spiritual exaltation, discretion and civility were alike forgotten, and I opened the door. What I saw took all philosophical speculation out of me in short order.

Moxon sat facing me at the farther side of a small table upon which a single candle made all the light that was in the room. Opposite him, his back toward me, sat another person. On the table between the two was a chess-board; the men were playing. I knew little of chess, but as only a few pieces were on the board it was obvious that the game was near its close. Moxon was intensely interested – not so much, it seemed to me, in the game as in his antagonist, upon whom he had fixed so intent a look that, standing though I did directly in the line of his vision, I was altogether unobserved. His face was ghastly white, and his eyes glittered like diamonds. Of his antagonist I had only a back view, but that was sufficient; I should not have cared to see his face.

He was apparently not more than five feet in height, with proportions suggesting those of a gorilla – a tremendous breadth of shoulders, thick, short neck and broad, squat head, which had a tangled growth of black hair and was topped with a crimson fez. A tunic of the same colour, belted tightly to the waist, reached the seat – apparently a box – upon which he sat; his legs and feet were not seen. His left forearm appeared to rest in his lap; he moved his pieces with his right hand, which seemed disproportionately long.

I had shrunk back and now stood a little to one side of the doorway and in shadow. If Moxon had looked farther than the face of his opponent he could have observed nothing now, except that the door was open. Something forbade me either to enter or to retire, a feeling – I know not how it came – that I was in the presence of an imminent tragedy and might serve my friend by remaining. With a scarcely conscious rebellion against the indelicacy of the act I remained.

The play was rapid. Moxon hardly glanced at the board before making his moves, and to my unskilled eye seemed to move the piece most convenient to his hand, his motions in doing so being quick, nervous and lacking in precision. The response of his antagonist, while equally prompt in the inception, was made with a slow, uniform, mechanical and, I thought, somewhat theatrical movement of the arm, that was a sore trial to my patience. There was something unearthly about it all, and I caught myself shuddering. But I was wet and cold.

Two or three times after moving a piece the stranger slightly inclined his head, and each time I observed that Moxon shifted his king. All at once the thought came to me that the man was dumb. And then that he was a machine – an automaton chess-player! Then I remembered that Moxon had once spoken to me of having invented such a piece of mechanism, though I did not understand that it had actually been constructed. Was all his talk about the consciousness and intelligence of machines merely a prelude to eventual exhibition of this device – only a trick to intensify the effect of its mechanical action upon me in my ignorance of its secret?

A fine end, this, of all my intellectual transports – my 'endless variety and excitement of philosophic thought'! I was about to retire in disgust when something occurred to hold my curiosity. I observed a shrug of the thing's great shoulders, as if it were irritated: and so natural was this – so entirely human – that in my new view of the matter it startled me. Nor was that all, for a moment later it struck the table sharply with its clenched hand. At that gesture Moxon seemed even more startled than I: he pushed his chair a little backward, as in alarm.

Presently Moxon, whose play it was, raised his hand high above the board, pounced upon one of his pieces like a sparrow-hawk and with the exclamation 'checkmate!' rose quickly to his feet and stepped behind his chair. The automaton sat motionless.

The wind had now gone down, but I heard, at lessening intervals and progressively louder, the rumble and roll of thunder. In the pauses between I now became conscious of a low humming or buzzing which, like the thunder, grew momentarily louder and more distinct. It seemed to come from the body of the automaton, and was unmistakably a whirring of wheels. It gave me the impression of a disordered mechanism which had escaped the repressive and regulating action of some controlling part – an effect such as might be expected if a pawl should be jostled from the teeth of a ratchet-wheel. But before I had time for much conjecture as to its nature my attention was taken by the strange motions of the automaton itself. A slight but continuous convulsion appeared to have possession of it. In body and head it shook like a man with palsy or an ague chill, and the motion augmented every moment until the entire figure was in violent agitation. Suddenly it sprang to its feet and with a movement almost too quick for the eye to follow shot forward across table and chair, with both arms thrust forth to their full length – the posture and lunge of a diver. Moxon tried to throw himself backward out of reach, but he was too late: I saw the horrible thing's hands close upon his throat, his own clutch its wrists. Then the table was overturned, the candle thrown to the floor and extinguished, and all was black dark. But the noise of the struggle was dreadfully distinct, and most terrible of all were the raucous, squawking sounds made by the strangled man's efforts to breathe. Guided by the infernal hubbub, I sprang to the rescue of my friend, but had hardly taken a stride in the darkness when the whole room blazed with a blinding white light that burned into my brain and heart and memory a vivid picture of the combatants on the floor, Moxon underneath, his throat still in the clutch of those iron hands, his head forced backward, his eyes protruding, his mouth wide open and his tongue thrust out; and – horrible contrast! – upon the painted face of his assassin an expression of tranquil and profound thought, as in the solution of a problem in chess! This I observed, then all was blackness and silence.

Three days later I recovered consciousness in a hospital. As the memory of that tragic night slowly evolved in my ailing brain I recognised in my attendant Moxon's confidential workman, Haley. Responding to a look he approached, smiling.

'Tell me about it,' I managed to say, faintly – 'all about it.'

'Certainly,' he said; 'you were carried unconscious from a burning house – Moxon's. Nobody knows how you came to be there. You may have to do a little explaining. The origin of the fire is a bit mysterious, too. My own notion is that the house was struck by lightning.'

'And Moxon?'

'Buried yesterday – what was left of him.'

Apparently this reticent person could unfold himself on occasion. When imparting shocking intelligence to the sick he was affable enough. After some moments of the keenest mental suffering I ventured to ask another question: 'Who rescued me?'

'Well, if that interests you – I did.'

'Thank you, Mr Haley, and may God bless you for it. Did you rescue, also, that charming product of your skill, the automaton chess-player that murdered its inventor?'

The man was silent a long time, looking away from me. Presently he turned and gravely said: 'Do you know that?'

'I do,' I replied; 'I saw it done.'

That was many years ago. If asked today I should answer less confidently.

A Tough Tussle

One night in the autumn of 1861 a man sat alone in the heart of a forest in western Virginia. The region was one of the wildest on the continent – the Cheat Mountain country. There was no lack of people close at hand, however; within a mile of where the man sat was the now silent camp of a whole Federal brigade. Somewhere about – it might be still nearer – was a force of the enemy, the numbers unknown. It was this uncertainty as to its numbers and position that accounted for the man's presence in that lonely spot; he was a young officer of a Federal infantry regiment and his business there was to guard his sleeping comrades in the camp against a surprise. He was in command of a detachment of men constituting a picket-guard. These men he had stationed just at nightfall in an irregular line, determined by the nature of the ground, several hundred yards in front of where he now sat. The line ran through the forest, among the rocks and laurel thickets, the men fifteen or twenty paces apart, all in concealment and under injunction of strict silence and unremitting vigilance. In four hours, if nothing occurred, they would be relieved by a fresh detachment from the reserve now resting in care of its captain some distance away to the left and rear. Before stationing his men the young officer of whom we are writing had pointed out to his two sergeants the spot at which he would be found if it should be necessary to consult him, or if his presence at the front line should be required.

It was a quiet enough spot – the fork of an old wood road, on the two branches of which, prolonging themselves deviously forward in the dim moonlight, the sergeants were themselves stationed, a few paces in rear of the line. If driven sharply back by a sudden onset of the enemy – and pickets are not expected to make a stand after firing – the men would come into the converging roads and naturally following them to their point of intersection could be rallied and 'formed'. In his small way the author of these dispositions was something of a strategist; if Napoleon had planned as intelligently at Waterloo he would have won that memorable battle and been overthrown later.

Second-Lieutenant Brainerd Byring was a brave and efficient officer, young and comparatively inexperienced as he was in the business of killing his fellow-men. He had enlisted in the very first days of the war as a private, with no military knowledge whatever, had been made first-sergeant of his company on account of his education and engaging manner, and had been lucky enough to lose his captain by a Confederate bullet; in the resulting promotions he had gained a commission. He had been in several engagements, such as they were – at Philippi, Rich Mountain, Carrick's Ford and Green-Brier – and had borne himself with such gallantry as not to attract the attention of his superior officers. The exhilaration of battle was agreeable to him, but the sight of the dead, with their clay faces, blank eyes and stiff bodies, which when not unnaturally shrunken were unnaturally swollen, had always intolerably affected him. He felt toward them a kind of reasonless antipathy that was something more than the physical and spiritual repugnance common to us all. Doubtless this feeling was due to his unusually acute sensibilities – his keen sense of the beautiful, which these hideous things outraged. Whatever may have been the cause, he could not look upon a dead body without a loathing which had in it an element of resentment. What others have respected as the dignity of death had to him no existence – was altogether unthinkable. Death was a thing to be hated. It was not picturesque, it had no tender and solemn side – a dismal thing, hideous in all its manifestations and suggestions. Lieutenant Byring was a braver man than anybody knew, for nobody knew his horror of that which he was ever ready to incur.

Having posted his men, instructed his sergeants and retired to his station, he seated himself on a log, and with senses all alert began his vigil. For greater ease he loosened his sword-belt and taking his heavy revolver from his holster laid it on the log beside him. He felt very comfortable, though he hardly gave the fact a thought, so intently did he listen for any sound from the front which might have a menacing significance – a shout, a shot, or the footfall of one of his sergeants coming to apprise him of something worth knowing. From the vast, invisible ocean of moonlight overhead fell, here and there, a slender, broken stream that seemed to splash against the intercepting branches and trickle to earth, forming small white pools among the clumps of laurel. But these leaks were few and served only to accentuate the blackness of his environment, which his imagination found it easy to people with all manner of unfamiliar shapes, menacing, uncanny, or merely grotesque.

He to whom the portentous conspiracy of night and solitude and silence in the heart of a great forest is not an unknown experience needs not to be told what another world it all is – how even the most commonplace and familiar objects take on another character. The trees group themselves differently; they draw closer together, as if in fear. The very silence has another quality than the silence of the day. And it is full of half-heard whispers – whispers that startle – ghosts of sounds long dead. There are living sounds, too, such as are never heard under other conditions: notes of strange night-birds, the cries of small animals in sudden encounters with stealthy foes or in their dreams, a rustling in the dead leaves – it may be the leap of a wood-rat, it may be the footfall of a panther. What caused the breaking of that twig? – what the low, alarmed twittering in that bushful of birds? There are sounds without a name, forms without substance, translations in space of objects which have not been seen to move, movements wherein nothing is observed to change its place. Ah, children of the sunlight and the gaslight, how little you know of the world in which you live!

Surrounded at a little distance by armed and watchful friends, Byring felt utterly alone. Yielding himself to the solemn and mysterious spirit of the time and place, he had forgotten the nature of his connection with the visible and audible aspects and phases of the night. The forest was boundless; men and the habitations of men did not exist. The universe was one primeval mystery of darkness, without form and void, himself the sole, dumb questioner of its eternal secret. Absorbed in thoughts born of this mood, he suffered the time to slip away unnoted. Meantime the infrequent patches of white light lying amongst the tree-trunks had undergone changes of size, form and place. In one of them nearby, just at the roadside, his eye fell upon an object that he had not previously observed. It was almost before his face as he sat; he could have sworn that it had not before been there. It was partly covered in shadow, but he could see that it was a human figure. Instinctively he adjusted the clasp of his sword-belt and laid hold of his pistol – again he was in a world of war, by occupation an assassin.

The figure did not move. Rising, pistol in hand, he approached. The figure lay upon its back, its upper part in shadow, but standing above it and looking down upon the face, he saw that it was a dead body. He shuddered and turned from it with a feeling of sickness and disgust, resumed his seat upon the log, and forgetting military prudence struck a match and lit a cigar. In the sudden blackness that followed the extinction of the flame he felt a sense of relief; he could no longer see the object of his aversion. Nevertheless, he kept his eyes in that direction until it appeared again with growing distinctness. It seemed to have moved a trifle nearer.

'Damn the thing!' he muttered. 'What does it want?'

It did not appear to be in need of anything but a soul.

Byring turned away his eyes and began humming a tune, but he broke off in the middle of a bar and looked at the dead body. Its presence annoyed him, though he could hardly have had a quieter neighbour. He was conscious, too, of a vague, indefinable feeling that was new to him. It was not fear, but rather a sense of the supernatural – in which he did not at all believe.

'I have inherited it,' he said to himself. 'I suppose it will require a thousand ages – perhaps ten thousand – for humanity to outgrow this feeling. Where and when did it originate? Away back, probably, in what is called the cradle of the human race – the plains of Central Asia. What we inherit as a superstition our barbarous ancestors must have held as a reasonable conviction. Doubtless they believed themselves justified by facts whose nature we cannot even conjecture in thinking a dead body a malign thing endowed with some strange power of mischief, with perhaps a will and a purpose to exert it. Possibly they had some awful form of religion of which that was one of the chief doctrines, sedulously taught by their priesthood, as ours teach the immortality of the soul. As the Aryans moved slowly on, to and through the Caucasus passes, and spread over Europe, new conditions of life must have resulted in the formulation of new religions. The old belief in the malevolence of the dead body was lost from the creeds and even perished from tradition, but it left its heritage of terror, which is transmitted from generation to generation – is as much a part of us as are our blood and bones.'

In following out his thought he had forgotten that which suggested it; but now his eye fell again upon the corpse. The shadow had now altogether uncovered it. He saw the sharp profile, the chin in the air, the whole face, ghastly white in the moonlight. The clothing was grey, the uniform of a Confederate soldier. The coat and waistcoat, unbuttoned, had fallen away on each side, exposing the white shirt. The chest seemed unnaturally prominent, but the abdomen had sunk in, leaving a sharp projection at the line of the lower ribs. The arms were extended, the left knee was thrust upward. The whole posture impressed Byring as having been studied with a view to the horrible.

'Bah!' he exclaimed; 'he was an actor – he knows how to be dead.'

He drew away his eyes, directing them resolutely along one of the roads leading to the front, and resumed his philosophising where he had left off.

'It may be that our Central Asian ancestors had not the custom of burial. In that case it is easy to understand their fear of the dead, who really were a menace and an evil. They bred pestilences. Children were taught to avoid the places where they lay, and to run away if by inadvertence they came near a corpse. I think, indeed, I'd better go away from this chap.'

He half rose to do so, then remembered that he had told his men in front and the officer in the rear who was to relieve him that he could at anytime be found at that spot. It was a matter of pride, too. If he abandoned his post he feared they would think he feared the corpse. He was no coward and he was unwilling to incur anybody's ridicule. So he again seated himself, and to prove his courage looked boldly at the body. The right arm – the one farthest from him – was now in shadow. He could hardly see the hand which, he had before observed, lay at the root of a clump of laurel. There had been no change, a fact which gave him a certain comfort, he could not have said why. He did not at once remove his eyes; that which we do not wish to see has a strange fascination, sometimes irresistible. Of the woman who covers her eyes with her hands and looks between the fingers let it be said that the wits have dealt with her not altogether justly.

Byring suddenly became conscious of a pain in his right hand. He withdrew his eyes from his enemy and looked at it. He was grasping the hilt of his drawn sword so tightly that it hurt him. He observed, too, that he was leaning forward in a strained attitude – crouching like a gladiator ready to spring at the throat of an antagonist. His teeth were clenched and he was breathing hard. This matter was soon set right, and as his muscles relaxed and he drew a long breath he felt keenly enough the ludicrousness of the incident. It affected him to laughter. Heavens! what sound was that? What mindless devil was uttering an unholy glee in mockery of human merriment? He sprang to his feet and looked about him, not recognising his own laugh.

He could no longer conceal from himself the horrible fact of his cowardice; he was thoroughly frightened! He would have run from the spot, but his legs refused their office; they gave way beneath him and he sat again upon the log, violently trembling. His face was wet, his whole body bathed in a chill perspiration. He could not even cry out. Distinctly he heard behind him a stealthy tread, as of some wild animal, and dared not look over his shoulder. Had the soulless living joined forces with the soulless dead? – was it an animal? Ah, if he could but be assured of that! But by no effort of will could he now unfix his gaze from the face of the dead man.

I repeat that Lieutenant Byring was a brave and intelligent man. But what would you have? Shall a man cope, single-handed, with so monstrous an alliance as that of night and solitude and silence and the dead, while an incalculable host of his own ancestors shriek into the ear of his spirit their coward counsel, sing their doleful death-songs in his heart, and disarm his very blood of all its iron? The odds are too great – courage was not made for so rough use as that.

One sole conviction now had the man in possession: that the body had moved. It lay nearer to the edge of its plot of light – there could be no doubt of it. It had also moved its arms, for, look, they are both in the shadow! A breath of cold air struck Byring full in the face; the boughs of trees above him stirred and moaned. A strongly defined shadow passed across the face of the dead, left it luminous, passed back upon it and left it half obscured. The horrible thing was visibly moving! At that moment a single shot rang out upon the picket-line – a lonelier and louder, though more distant, shot than ever had been heard by mortal ear! It broke the spell of that enchanted man; it slew the silence and the solitude, dispersed the hindering host from Central Asia and released his modern manhood. With a cry like that of some great bird pouncing upon its prey he sprang forward, hot-hearted for action!

Shot after shot now came from the front. There were shoutings and confusion, hoof-beats and desultory cheers. Away to the rear, in the sleeping camp, were a singing of bugles and grumble of drums. Pushing through the thickets on either side the roads came the Federal pickets, in full retreat, firing backward at random as they ran. A straggling group that had followed back one of the roads, as instructed, suddenly sprang away into the bushes as half a hundred horsemen thundered by them, striking wildly with their sabres as they passed. At headlong speed these mounted madmen shot past the spot where Byring had sat, and vanished round an angle of the road, shouting and firing their pistols. A moment later there was a roar of musketry, followed by dropping shots – they had encountered the reserve-guard in line; and back they came in dire confusion, with here and there an empty saddle and many a maddened horse, bullet-stung, snorting and plunging with pain. It was all over – 'an affair of outposts'.

The line was re-established with fresh men, the roll called, the stragglers were re-formed. The Federal commander, with a part of his staff, imperfectly clad, appeared upon the scene, asked a few questions, looked exceedingly wise and retired. After standing at arms for an hour the brigade in camp 'swore a prayer or two' and went to bed.

Early the next morning a fatigue-party, commanded by a captain and accompanied by a surgeon, searched the ground for dead and wounded. At the fork of the road, a little to one side, they found two bodies lying close together – that of a Federal officer and that of a Confederate private. The officer had died of a sword-thrust through the heart, but not, apparently, until he had inflicted upon his enemy no fewer than five dreadful wounds. The dead officer lay on his face in a pool of blood, the weapon still in his heart. They turned him on his back and the surgeon removed it.

'Gad!' said the captain – 'It is Byring!' – adding, with a glance at the other, 'They had a tough tussle.'

The surgeon was examining the sword. It was that of a line officer of Federal infantry – exactly like the one worn by the captain. It was, in fact, Byring's own. The only other weapon discovered was an undischarged revolver in the dead officer's belt.

The surgeon laid down the sword and approached the other body. It was frightfully gashed and stabbed, but there was no blood. He took hold of the left foot and tried to straighten the leg. In the effort the body was displaced. The dead do not wish to be moved – it protested with a faint, sickening odour. Where it had lain were a few maggots, manifesting an imbecile activity.

The surgeon looked at the captain. The captain looked at the surgeon.

One of Twins

A Letter found among the Papers of the late Mortimer Barr

You ask me if in my experience as one of a pair of twins I ever observed anything unaccountable by the natural laws with which we have acquaintance. As to that you shall judge; perhaps we have not all acquaintance with the same natural laws. You may know some that I do not, and what is to me unaccountable may be very clear to you.

You knew my brother John – that is, you knew him when you knew that I was not present; but neither you nor I, I believe, any human being could distinguish between him and me if we chose to seem alike. Our parents could not; ours is the only instance of which I have any knowledge of so close resemblance as that. I speak of my brother John, but I am not at all sure that his name was not Henry and mine John. We were regularly christened, but afterward, in the very act of tattooing us with small distinguishing marks, the operator lost his reckoning; and although I bear upon my forearm a small 'H' and he bore a 'J', it is by no means certain that the letters ought not to have been transposed. During our boyhood our parents tried to distinguish us more obviously by our clothing and other simple devices, but we would so frequently exchange suits and otherwise circumvent the enemy that they abandoned all such ineffectual attempts, and during all the years that we lived together at home everybody recognised the difficulty of the situation and made the best of it by calling us both 'Jehnry'. I have often wondered at my father's forbearance in not branding us conspicuously upon our unworthy brows, but as we were tolerably good boys and used our power of embarrassment and annoyance with commendable moderation, we escaped the iron. My father was, in fact, a singularly good-natured man, and I think quietly enjoyed Nature's practical joke.

Soon after we had come to California, and settled at San Jose (where the only good fortune that awaited us was our meeting with so kind a friend as you), the family, as you know, was broken up by the death of both my parents in the same week. My father died insolvent, and the homestead was sacrificed to pay his debts. My sisters returned to relatives in the East, but owing to your kindness, John and I, then twenty-two years of age, obtained employment in San Francisco, in different quarters of the town. Circumstances did not permit us to live together, and we saw each other infrequently, sometimes not oftener than once a week. As we had few acquaintances in common, the fact of our extraordinary likeness was little known. I come now to the matter of your inquiry.

One day soon after we had come to this city I was walking down Market Street late in the afternoon, when I was accosted by a well-dressed man of middle age, who after greeting me cordially said: 'Stevens, I know, of course, that you do not go out much, but I have told my wife about you, and she would be glad to see you at the house. I have a notion, too, that my girls are worth knowing. Suppose you come out tomorrow at six and dine with us, *en famille*; and then if the ladies can't amuse you afterward I'll stand in with a few games of billiards.'

This was said with so bright a smile and so engaging a manner that I had not the heart to refuse, and although I had never seen the man in my life I promptly replied: 'You are very good, sir, and it will give me great pleasure to accept the invitation. Please present my compliments to Mrs Margovan and ask her to expect me.'

With a shake of the hand and a pleasant parting word the man passed on. That he had mistaken me for my brother was plain enough. That was an error to which I was accustomed and which it was not my habit to rectify unless the matter seemed important. But how had I known that this man's name was Margovan? It certainly is not a name that one would apply to a man at random, with a probability that it would be right. In point of fact, the name was as strange to me as the man.

The next morning I hastened to where my brother was employed and met him coming out of the office with a number of bills that he was to collect. I told him how I had 'committed' him and added that if he didn't care to keep the engagement I should be delighted to continue the impersonation.

'That's queer,' he said thoughtfully. 'Margovan is the only man in the office here whom I know well and like. When he came in this morning and we had passed the usual greetings some singular impulse prompted me to say: "Oh, I beg your pardon, Mr Margovan, but I neglected to ask your address." I got the address, but what under the sun I was to do with it, I did not know until now. It's good of you to offer to take the consequence of your impudence, but I'll eat that dinner myself, if you please.'

He ate a number of dinners at the same place – more than were good for him, I may add without disparaging their quality; for he fell in love with Miss Margovan, proposed marriage to her and was heartlessly accepted.

Several weeks after I had been informed of the engagement, but before it had been convenient for me to make the acquaintance of the young woman and her family, I met one day on Kearney Street a handsome but somewhat dissipated-looking man whom something prompted me to follow and watch, which I did without any scruple whatever. He turned up Geary Street and followed it until he came to Union Square. There he looked at his watch, then entered the square. He loitered about the paths for some time, evidently waiting for someone. Presently he was joined by a fashionably dressed and beautiful young woman and the two walked away up Stockton Street, I following. I now felt the necessity of extreme caution, for although the girl was a stranger it seemed to me that she would recognise me at a glance. They made several turns from one street to another and finally, after both had taken a hasty look all about – which I narrowly evaded by stepping into a doorway – they entered a house of which I do not care to state the location. Its location was better than its character.

I protest that my action in playing the spy upon these two strangers was without assignable motive. It was one of which I might or might not be ashamed, according to my estimate of the character of the person finding it out. As an essential part of a narrative educed by your question it is related here without hesitancy or shame.

A week later John took me to the house of his prospective father-in-law, and in Miss Margovan, as you have already surmised, but to my profound astonishment, I recognised the heroine of that discreditable adventure. A gloriously beautiful heroine of a discreditable adventure I must in justice admit that she was; but that fact has only this importance: her beauty was such a surprise to me that it cast a doubt upon her identity with the young woman I had seen before; how could the marvellous fascination of her face have failed to strike me at that time? But no – there was no possibility of error; the difference was due to costume, light and general surroundings.

John and I passed the evening at the house, enduring, with the fortitude of long experience, such delicate enough banter as our likeness naturally suggested. When the young lady and I were left alone for a few minutes I looked her squarely in the face and said with sudden gravity:

'You, too, Miss Margovan, have a double: I saw her last Tuesday afternoon in Union Square.'

She trained her great grey eyes upon me for a moment, but her glance was a trifle less steady than my own and she withdrew it, fixing it on the tip of her shoe.

'Was she very like me?' she asked, with an indifference which I thought a little overdone.

'So like,' said I, 'that I greatly admired her, and being unwilling to lose sight of her I confess that I followed her until – Miss Margovan, are you sure that you understand?'

She was now pale, but entirely calm. She again raised her eyes to mine, with a look that did not falter.

'What do you wish me to do?' she asked. 'You need not fear to name your terms. I accept them.'

It was plain, even in the brief time given me for reflection, that in dealing with this girl ordinary methods would not do, and ordinary exactions were needless.

'Miss Margovan,' I said, doubtless with something of the compassion in my voice that I had in my heart, 'it is impossible not to think you the victim of some horrible compulsion. Rather than impose new embarrassments upon you I would prefer to aid you to regain your freedom.

She shook her head, sadly and hopelessly, and I continued, with agitation:

'Your beauty unnerves me. I am disarmed by your frankness and your distress. If you are free to act upon conscience you will, I believe, do what you conceive to be best; if you are not – well, Heaven help us all! You have nothing to fear from me but such opposition to this marriage as I can try to justify on – on other grounds.'

These were not my exact words, but that was the sense of them, as nearly as my sudden and conflicting emotions permitted me to express it. I rose and left her without another look at her, met the others as they re-entered the room and said, as calmly as I could: 'I have been bidding Miss Margovan good-evening; it is later than I thought.'

John decided to go with me. In the street he asked if I had observed anything singular in Julia's manner.

'I thought her ill,' I replied; 'that is why I left.' Nothing more was said.

The next evening I came late to my lodgings. The events of the previous evening had made me nervous and ill; I had tried to cure myself and attain to clear thinking by walking in the open air, but I was oppressed with a horrible presentiment of evil – a presentiment which I could not formulate. It was a chill, foggy night; my clothing and hair were damp and I shook with cold. In my dressing-gown and slippers before a blazing grate of coals I was even more uncomfortable. I no longer shivered but shuddered – there is a difference. The dread of some impending calamity was so strong and dispiriting that I tried to drive it away by inviting a real sorrow – tried to dispel the conception of a terrible future by substituting the memory of a painful past. I recalled the death of my parents and endeavoured to fix my mind upon the last sad scenes at their bedsides and their graves. It all seemed vague and unreal, as having occurred ages ago and to another person. Suddenly, striking through my thought and parting it as a tense cord is parted by the stroke of steel – I can think of no other comparison – I heard a sharp cry as of one in mortal agony! The voice was that of my brother and seemed to come from the street outside my window. I sprang to the window and threw it open. A street lamp directly opposite threw a wan and ghastly light upon the wet pavement and the fronts of the houses. A single policeman, with upturned collar, was leaning against a gatepost, quietly smoking a cigar. No one else was in sight. I closed the window and pulled down the shade, seated myself before the fire and tried to fix my mind upon my surroundings. By way of assisting, by performance of some familiar act, I looked at my watch; it marked half-past eleven. Again I heard that awful cry! It seemed in the room – at my side. I was frightened and for some moments had not the power to move. A few minutes later – I have no recollection of the intermediate time – I found myself hurrying along an unfamiliar street as fast as I could walk. I did not know where I was, nor whither I was going, but presently sprang up the steps of a house before which were two or three carriages and in which were moving lights and a subdued confusion of voices. It was the house of Mr Margovan.

You know, good friend, what had occurred there. In one chamber lay Julia Margovan, hours dead by poison; in another John Stevens, bleeding from a pistol wound in the chest, inflicted by his own hand. As I burst into the room, pushed aside the physicians and laid my hand upon his forehead he unclosed his eyes, stared blankly, closed them slowly and died without a sign.

I knew no more until six weeks afterwards, when I had been nursed back to life by your own saintly wife in your own beautiful home. All of that you know, but what you do not know is this – which, however, has no bearing upon the subject of your psychological researches – at least not upon that branch of them in which, with a delicacy and consideration all your own, you have asked for less assistance than I think I have given you:

One moonlight night several years afterward I was passing through Union Square. The hour was late and the square deserted. Certain memories of the past naturally came into my mind as I came to the spot where I had once witnessed that fateful assignation, and with that unaccountable perversity which prompts us to dwell upon thoughts of the most painful character I seated myself upon one of the benches to indulge them. A man entered the square and came along the walk toward me. His hands were clasped behind him, his head was bowed; he seemed to observe nothing. As he approached the shadow in which I sat I recognised him as the man whom I had seen meet Julia Margovan years before at that spot. But he was terribly altered – grey, worn and haggard. Dissipation and vice were in evidence in every look; illness was no less apparent. His clothing was in disorder, his hair fell across his forehead in a derangement which was at once uncanny, and picturesque. He looked fitter for restraint than liberty – the restraint of a hospital.

With no defined purpose I rose and confronted him. He raised his head and looked me full in the face. I have no words to describe the ghastly change that came over his own; it was a look of unspeakable terror – he thought himself eye to eye with a ghost. But he was a courageous man. 'Damn you, John Stevens!' he cried, and lifting his trembling arm he dashed his fist feebly at my face and fell headlong upon the gravel as I walked away.

Somebody found him there, stone dead. Nothing more is known of him, not even his name. To know of a man that he is dead should be enough.

The Haunted Valley

How Trees are Felled in China

A half-mile north from Joe Dunfer's, on the road from Hutton's to Mexican Hill, the highway dips into a sunless ravine which opens out on either hand in a half-confidential manner, as if it had a secret to impart at some more convenient season. I never used to ride through it without looking first to the one side and then to the other, to see if the time had arrived for the revelation. If I saw nothing – and I never did see anything – there was no feeling of disappointment, for I knew the disclosure was merely withheld temporarily for some good reason which I had no right to question. That I should one day be taken into full confidence I no more doubted than I doubted the existence of Joe Dunfer himself, through whose premises the ravine ran.

It was said that Joe had once undertaken to erect a cabin in some remote part of it, but for some reason had abandoned the enterprise and constructed his present hermaphrodite habitation, half residence and half groggery, at the roadside, upon an extreme corner of his estate; as far away as possible, as if on purpose to show how radically he had changed his mind.

This Joe Dunfer – or, as he was familiarly known in the neighbourhood, Whisky Joe – was a very important personage in those parts. He was apparently about forty years of age, a long, shock-headed fellow, with a corded face, a gnarled arm and a knotty hand like a bunch of prison-keys. He was a hairy man, with a stoop in his walk, like that of one who is about to spring upon something and rend it.

Next to the peculiarity to which he owed his local appellation, Mr Dunfer's most obvious characteristic was a deep-seated antipathy to the Chinese. I saw him once in a towering rage because one of his herdsmen had permitted a travel-heated Asian to slake his thirst at the horse-trough in front of the saloon end of Joe's establishment. I ventured faintly to remonstrate with Joe for his unchristian spirit, but he merely explained that there was nothing about Chinamen in the New Testament, and strode away to wreak his displeasure upon his dog, which also, I suppose, the inspired scribes had overlooked.

Some days afterward, finding him sitting alone in his bar-room, I cautiously approached the subject, when, greatly to my relief, the habitual austerity of his expression visibly softened into something that I took for condescension.

'You young Easterners,' he said, 'are a mile and a half too good for this country, and you don't catch on to our play. People who don't know a Chileño from a Kanaka can afford to hang out liberal ideas about Chinese immigration, but a fellow that has to fight for his bone with a lot of mongrel coolies hasn't anytime for foolishness.'

This long consumer, who had probably never done an honest day's work in his life, sprung the lid of a Chinese tobacco-box and with thumb and forefinger forked out a wad like a small haycock. Holding this reinforcement within supporting distance he fired away with renewed confidence.

'They're a flight of devouring locusts, and they're going for everything green in this God blest land, if you want to know.'

Here he pushed his reserve into the breach and when his gabble-gear was again disengaged resumed his uplifting discourse.

'I had one of them on this ranch five years ago, and I'll tell you about it, so that you can see the nub of this whole question. I didn't pan out particularly well those days – drank more whisky than was prescribed for me and didn't seem to care for my duty as a patriotic American citizen; so I took that pagan in, as a kind of cook. But when I got religion over at the Hill and they talked of running me for the Legislature it was given to me to see the light. But what was I to do? If I gave him the go somebody else would take him, and mightn't treat him white. *What* was I to do? What would any good Christian do, especially one new to the trade and full to the neck with the brotherhood of Man and the fatherhood of God?'

Joe paused for a reply, with an expression of unstable satisfaction, as of one who has solved a problem by a distrusted method. Presently he rose and swallowed a glass of whisky from a full bottle on the counter, then resumed his story.

'Besides, he didn't count for much – didn't know anything and gave himself airs. They all do that. I said him nay, but he muled it through on that line while he lasted; but after turning the other cheek seventy and seven times I doctored the dice so that he didn't last for ever. And I'm almighty glad I had the sand to do it.'

Joe's gladness, which somehow did not impress me, was duly and ostentatiously celebrated at the bottle.

'About five years ago I started in to stick up a shack. That was before this one was built, and I put it in another place. I set Ah Wee and a little cuss named Gopher to cutting the timber. Of course I didn't expect Ah Wee to help much, for he had a face like a day in June and big black eyes – I guess maybe they were the damn'dest eyes in this neck o' woods.'

While delivering this trenchant thrust at common sense Mr Dunfer absently regarded a knot-hole in the thin board partition separating the bar from the living-room, as if that were one of the eyes whose size and colour had incapacitated his servant for good service.

'Now you Eastern galoots won't believe anything against the yellow devils,' he suddenly flamed out with an appearance of earnestness not altogether convincing, 'but I tell you that Chink was the perversest scoundrel outside San Francisco. The miserable pig-tail Mongolian went to hewing away at the saplings all round the stems, like a worm o' the dust gnawing a radish. I pointed out his error as patiently as I knew how, and showed him how to cut them on two sides, so as to make them fall right; but no sooner would I turn my back on him, like this' – and he turned it on me, amplifying the illustration by taking some more liquor – 'than he was at it again. It was just this way: while I looked at him, *so* – regarding me rather unsteadily and with evident complexity of vision – 'he was all right; but when I looked away, *so* – taking a long pull at the bottle – 'he defied me. Then I'd gaze at him reproachfully, *so*, and butter wouldn't have melted in his mouth.'

Doubtless Mr Dunfer honestly intended the look that he fixed upon me to be merely reproachful, but it was singularly fit to arouse the gravest apprehension in any unarmed person incurring it; and as I had lost all interest in his pointless and interminable narrative, I rose to go. Before I had fairly risen, he had again turned to the counter, and with a barely audible 'so', had emptied the bottle at a gulp.

Heavens! what a yell! It was like a Titan in his last, strong agony. Joe staggered back after emitting it, as a cannon recoils from its own thunder, and then dropped into his chair, as if he had been 'knocked in the head' like a beef – his eyes drawn sidewise toward the wall, with a stare of terror. Looking in the same direction, I saw that the knot-hole in the wall had indeed become a human eye – a full, black eye, that glared into my own with an entire lack of expression more awful than the most devilish glitter. I think I must have covered my face with my hands to shut out the horrible illusion, if such it was, and Joe's little white man-of-all-work coming into the room broke the spell, and I walked out of the house with a sort of dazed fear that *delirium tremens* might be infectious. My horse was hitched at the watering-trough, and untying him I mounted and gave him his head, too much troubled in mind to note whither he took me.

I did not know what to think of all this, and like everyone who does not know what to think I thought a great deal, and to little purpose. The only reflection that seemed at all satisfactory was, that on the morrow I should be some miles away, with a strong probability of never returning.

A sudden coolness brought me out of my abstraction, and looking up I found myself entering the deep shadows of the ravine. The day was stifling; and this transition from pitiless, visible heat of the parched fields to the cool gloom, heavy with pungency of cedars and vocal with twittering of the birds that had been driven to its leafy asylum, was exquisitely refreshing. I looked for my mystery, as usual, but not finding the ravine in a communicative mood, dismounted, led my sweating animal into the undergrowth, tied him securely to a tree and sat down upon a rock to meditate.

I began bravely by analysing my pet superstition about the place. Having resolved it into its constituent elements I arranged them in convenient troops and squadrons, and collecting all the forces of my logic bore down upon them from impregnable premises with the thunder of irresistible conclusions and a great noise of chariots and general intellectual shouting. Then, when my big mental guns had overturned all opposition, and were growling almost inaudibly away on the horizon of pure speculation, the routed enemy straggled in upon their rear, massed silently into a solid phalanx, and captured me, bag and baggage. An indefinable dread came upon me. I rose to shake it off, and began threading the narrow dell by an old, grass-grown cow-path that seemed to flow along the bottom, as a substitute for the brook that Nature had neglected to provide.

The trees among which the path straggled were ordinary, well-behaved plants, a trifle perverted as to trunk and eccentric as to bough, but with nothing unearthly in their general aspect. A few loose boulders, which had detached themselves from the sides of the depression to set up an independent existence at the bottom, had dammed up the pathway, here and there, but their stony repose had nothing in it of the stillness of death. There was a kind of death-chamber hush in the valley, it is true, and a mysterious whisper above: the wind was just fingering the tops of the trees – that was all.

I had not thought of connecting Joe Dunfer's drunken narrative with what I now sought, and only when I came into a clear space and stumbled over the level trunks of some small trees did I have the revelation. This was the site of the abandoned 'shack'. The discovery was verified by noting that some of the rotting stumps were hacked all round, in a most unwoodman-like way, while others were cut straight across, and the butt ends of the corresponding trunks had the blunt wedge-form given by the axe of a master.

The opening among the trees was not more than thirty paces across. At one side was a little knoll – a natural hillock, bare of shrubbery but covered with wild grass, and on this, standing out of the grass, the headstone of a grave!

I do not remember that I felt anything like surprise at this discovery. I viewed that lonely grave with something of the feeling that Columbus must have had when he saw the hills and headlands of the new world. Before approaching it I leisurely completed my survey of the surroundings. I was even guilty of the affectation of winding my watch at that unusual hour, and with needless care and deliberation. Then I approached my mystery.

The grave – a rather short one – was in somewhat better repair than was consistent with its obvious age and isolation, and my eyes, I dare say, widened a trifle at a clump of unmistakable garden flowers showing evidence of recent watering. The stone had clearly enough done duty once as a doorstep. In its front was carved, or rather dug, an inscription. It read thus:

AH WEE — CHINAMAN

AGE UNKNOWN
WORKED FOR JOE DUNFER

THIS MONUMENT IS ERECTED BY HIM
TO KEEP THE CHINK'S
MEMORY GREEN.
LIKEWISE AS A WARNING TO CELESTIALS
NOT TO TAKE ON AIRS. DEVIL TAKE 'EM!
SHE WAS A GOOD EGG.

I cannot adequately relate my astonishment at this uncommon inscription! The meagre but sufficient identification of the deceased;

the impudent candour of confession; the brutal anathema; the ludicrous change of sex and sentiment – all marked this record as the work of one who must have been at least as much demented as bereaved. I felt that any further disclosure would be a paltry anti-climax, and with an unconscious regard for dramatic effect turned squarely about and walked away. Nor did I return to that part of the county for four years.

❧ TWO ❧

Who Drives Sane Oxen should Himself be Sane

'Gee-up, there, old Fuddy-Duddy!'

This unique adjuration came from the lips of a queer little man perched upon a wagonful of firewood, behind a brace of oxen that were hauling it easily along with a simulation of mighty effort which had evidently not imposed on their lord and master. As that gentleman happened at the moment to be staring me squarely in the face as I stood by the roadside it was not altogether clear whether he was addressing me or his beasts; nor could I say if they were named Fuddy and Duddy and were both subjects of the imperative mood to 'gee-up'. Anyhow the command produced no effect on us, and the queer little man removed his eyes from mine long enough to spear Fuddy and Duddy alternately with a long pole, remarking, quietly but with feeling: 'Dern your skin,' as if they enjoyed that integument in common. Observing that my request for a ride took no attention, and finding myself falling slowly astern, I placed one foot upon the inner circumference of a hind wheel and was slowly elevated to the level of the hub, whence I boarded the concern, *sans cérémonie*, and scrambling forward seated myself beside the driver – who took no notice of me until he had administered another indiscriminate castigation to his cattle, accompanied with the advice to 'buckle down, you derned Incapable!' Then, the master of the outfit (or rather the former master, for I could not suppress a whimsical feeling that the entire establishment was my lawful prize) trained his big, black eyes upon me with an expression strangely, and somewhat unpleasantly, familiar, laid down his rod – which neither blossomed nor turned into a serpent, as I half expected – folded his arms, and gravely demanded, 'W'at did you do to W'isky?'

My natural reply would have been that I drank it, but there was something about the query that suggested a hidden significance, and something about the man that did not invite a shallow jest. And so, having no other answer ready, I merely held my tongue, but felt as if I were resting under an imputation of guilt, and that my silence was being construed into a confession.

Just then a cold shadow fell upon my cheek, and caused me to look up. We were descending into my ravine! I cannot describe the sensation that came upon me: I had not seen it since it unbosomed itself four years before, and now I felt like one to whom a friend has made some sorrowing confession of crime long past, and who has basely deserted him in consequence. The old memories of Joe Dunfer, his fragmentary revelation, and the unsatisfying explanatory note by the headstone, came back with singular distinctness. I wondered what had become of Joe, and – I turned sharply round and asked my prisoner. He was intently watching his cattle, and without withdrawing his eyes replied:

'Gee-up, old Terrapin! He lies aside of Ah Wee up the gulch. Like to see it? They always come back to the spot – I've been expectin' you. H-woa!'

At the enunciation of the aspirate, Fuddy-Duddy, the incapable terrapin, came to a dead halt, and before the vowel had died away up the ravine had folded up all his eight legs and lain down in the dusty road, regardless of the effect upon his derned skin. The queer little man slid off his seat to the ground and started up the dell without deigning to look back to see if I was following. But I was.

It was about the same season of the year, and at near the same hour of the day, of my last visit. The jays clamoured loudly, and the trees whispered darkly, as before; and I somehow traced in the two sounds a fanciful analogy to the open boastfulness of Mr Joe Dunfer's mouth and the mysterious reticence of his manner, and to the mingled hardihood and tenderness of his sole literary production – the epitaph. All things in the valley seemed unchanged, excepting the cow-path, which was almost wholly overgrown with weeds. When we came out into the 'clearing', however, there was change enough. Among the stumps and trunks of the fallen saplings, those that had been hacked 'China fashion' were no longer distinguishable from those that were cut ' 'Melican way'. It was as if the Old-World barbarism and the New-World civilisation had reconciled their differences by the arbitration of an impartial decay – as is the way of civilisations. The knoll was there, but the Hunnish brambles had overrun and all but obliterated its effete grasses; and the patrician garden-violet had capitulated to his plebeian brother – perhaps had merely reverted to his original type. Another grave – a long, robust mound – had been made beside the first, which seemed to shrink from the comparison; and in the shadow of a new headstone the old one lay prostrate, with its marvellous inscription illegible by accumulation of leaves and soil. In point of literary merit the new was inferior to the old – was even repulsive in its terse and savage jocularity:

JOE DUNFER. DONE FOR.

I turned from it with indifference, and brushing away the leaves from the tablet of the dead pagan restored to light the mocking words which, fresh from their long neglect, seemed to have a certain pathos. My guide, too, appeared to take on an added seriousness as he read it, and I fancied that I could detect beneath his whimsical manner something of manliness, almost of dignity. But while I looked at him his former aspect, so subtly unhuman, so tantalisingly familiar, crept back into his big eyes, repellent and attractive. I resolved to make an end of the mystery if possible.

'My friend,' I said, pointing to the smaller grave, 'did Joe Dunfer murder that Chinaman?'

He was leaning against a tree and looking across the open space into the top of another, or into the blue sky beyond. He neither withdrew his eyes, nor altered his posture as he slowly replied:

'No, sir; he justifiably homicided him.'

'Then he really did kill him.'

'Kill 'im? I should say he did, rather. Doesn't everybody know that? Didn't he stan' up before the coroner's jury and confess it? And didn't they find a verdict of "Came to 'is death by a wholesome Christian sentiment workin' in the Caucasian breast"? An' didn't the church at the Hill turn W'isky down for it? And didn't the sovereign people elect him Justice of the Peace to get even on the gospellers? I don't know where you were brought up.'

'But did Joe do that because the Chinaman did not, or would not, learn to cut down trees like a white man?'

'Sure! – it stan's so on the record, which makes it true an' legal. My knowin' better doesn't make any difference with legal truth; it wasn't my funeral and I wasn't invited to deliver an oration. But the fact is, W'isky was jealous o' *me*' – and the little wretch actually swelled out like a turkeycock and made a pretence of adjusting an imaginary neck-tie, noting the effect in the palm of his hand, held up before him to represent a mirror.

'Jealous of *you*!' I repeated with ill-mannered astonishment.

'That's what I said. Why not? – don't I look all right?'

He assumed a mocking attitude of studied grace, and twitched the wrinkles out of his threadbare waistcoat.

Then, suddenly dropping his voice to a low pitch of singular sweetness, he continued: 'W'isky thought a lot o' that Chink; nobody but me knew how 'e doted on 'im. Couldn't bear 'im out of 'is sight, the derned protoplasm! And w'en 'e came down to this clearin' one day an' found 'im an' me neglectin' our work – 'im asleep an' me grapplin' a tarantula out of 'is sleeve – W'isky laid hold of my axe and let us have it, good an' hard! I dodged just then, for the spider bit me, but Ah Wee got it bad in the side an' tumbled about like anything. W'isky was just weighin' me out one w'en 'e saw the spider fastened on my finger; then 'e knew 'e'd made a jackass of 'imself. 'E threw away the axe and got down on 'is knees alongside of Ah Wee, who gave a last little kick and opened 'is eyes – 'e had eyes like mine – an' puttin' up 'is hands drew down W'isky's ugly head and held it there w'ile 'e stayed. That wasn't long, for a tremblin' ran through 'im and 'e gave a bit of a moan an' beat the game.'

During the progress of the story the narrator had become transfigured. The comic, or rather, the sardonic element was all out of him, and as he painted that strange scene it was with difficulty that I kept my composure. And this consummate actor had somehow so managed me that the sympathy due to his *dramatis personae* was given to himself. I stepped forward to grasp his hand, when suddenly a broad grin danced across his face and with a light, mocking laugh he continued: 'W'en W'isky got 'is nut out o' that 'e was a sight to see! All 'is fine clothes – 'e dressed mighty blindin' those days – were spoiled everlastin'! 'Is hair was tousled and 'is face – what I could see of it – was whiter than the ace of lilies. 'E stared once at me, and looked away as if I didn't count; an' then there were shootin' pains chasin' one another from my bitten finger into my head, and it was Gopher to the dark. That's why I wasn't at the inquest.'

'But why did you hold your tongue afterward?' I asked.

'It's that kind of tongue,' he replied, and not another word would he say about it.

'After that W'isky took to drinkin' harder an' harder, and was rabider an' rabider anti-coolie, but I don't think 'e was ever particularly glad that 'e dispelled Ah Wee. 'E didn't put on so much dog about it w'en we were alone as w'en 'e had the ear of a derned Spectacular Extravaganza like you. 'E put up that headstone and gouged the inscription accordin' to 'is varyin' moods. It took 'im three weeks, workin' between drinks. I gouged 'is in one day.'

'When did Joe die?' I asked rather absently.

The answer took my breath: 'Pretty soon after I looked at 'im through that knothole, w'en you had put something in 'is w'isky, you derned Borgia!'

Recovering somewhat from my surprise at this astounding charge, I was half-minded to throttle the audacious accuser, but was restrained by a sudden conviction that came to me in the light of a revelation. I fixed a grave look upon him and asked, as calmly as I could: 'And when did you go loony?'

'Nine years ago!' he shrieked, throwing out his clenched hands – 'nine years ago, w'en that big brute killed the woman who loved him better than she did me! – me who had followed 'er from San Francisco, where 'e won 'er at draw poker! – me who had watched over 'er for years w'en the scoundrel she belonged to was ashamed to acknowledge 'er and treat 'er white! – me who for her sake kept 'is cussed secret till it ate 'im up! – me who w'en you poisoned the beast fulfilled 'is last request to lay 'im alongside 'er and give 'im a stone to the head of 'im! And I've never since seen 'er grave till now, for I didn't want to meet 'im here.'

'Meet him? Why, Gopher, my poor fellow, he is dead!'

'That's why I'm afraid of 'im.'

I followed the little wretch back to his wagon and wrung his hand at parting. It was now nightfall, and as I stood there at the roadside in the deepening gloom, watching the blank outlines of the receding wagon, a sound was borne to me on the evening wind – a sound as of a series of vigorous thumps – and a voice came out of the night: 'Gee-up, there, you derned old Geranium.'

A Jug of Syrup

This narrative begins with the death of its hero. Silas Deemer died on the 16th day of July, 1874, and two days later his remains were buried. As he had been personally known to every man, woman and well-grown child in the village, the funeral, as the local newspaper phrased it, 'was largely attended'. In accordance with a custom of the time and place, the coffin was opened at the graveside and the entire assembly of friends and neighbours filed past, taking a last look at the face of the dead. And then, before the eyes of all, Silas Deemer was put into the ground. Some of the eyes were a trifle dim, but in a general way it may be said that at that interment there was lack of neither observance nor observation; Silas was indubitably dead, and none could have pointed out any ritual delinquency that would have justified him in coming back from the grave. Yet if human testimony is good for anything (and certainly it once put an end to witchcraft in and about Salem) he came back.

I forgot to state that the death and burial of Silas Deemer occurred in the little village of Hillbrook, where he had lived for thirty-one years. He had been what is known in some parts of the Union (which is admittedly a free country) as a 'merchant'; that is to to say, he kept a retail shop for the sale of such things as are commonly sold in shops of that character. His honesty had never been questioned, so far as is known, and he was held in high esteem by all. The only thing that could be urged against him by the most censorious was a too close attention to business. It was not urged against him, though many another, who manifested it in no greater degree, was less leniently judged. The business to which Silas was devoted was mostly his own – that, possibly, may have made a difference.

At the time of Deemer's death nobody could recollect a single day, Sundays excepted, that he had not passed in his 'store', since he had opened it more than a quarter-century before. His health having been perfect during all that time, he had been unable to discern any validity in whatever may or might have been urged to lure him astray from his counter; and it is related that once when he was summoned to the county seat as a witness in an important law case and did not attend, the lawyer who had the hardihood to move that he be 'admonished' was solemnly informed that the Court regarded the proposal with 'surprise'. Judicial surprise being an emotion that attorneys are not commonly ambitious to arouse, the motion was hastily withdrawn and an agreement with the other side effected as to what Mr Deemer would have said if he had been there – the other side pushing its advantage to the extreme and making the supposititious testimony distinctly damaging to the interests of its proponents. In brief, it was the general feeling in all that region that Silas Deemer was the one immobile verity of Hillbrook, and that his translation in space would precipitate some dismal public ill or strenuous calamity.

Mrs Deemer and two grown daughters occupied the upper rooms of the building, but Silas had never been known to sleep elsewhere than on a cot behind the counter of the store. And there, quite by accident, he was found one night, dying, and passed away just before the time for taking down the shutters. Though speechless, he appeared conscious, and it was thought by those who knew him best that if the end had unfortunately been delayed beyond the usual hour for opening the store the effect upon him would have been deplorable.

Such had been Silas Deemer – such the fixity and invariety of his life and habit, that the village humorist (who had once attended college) was moved to bestow upon him the sobriquet of 'Old Ibidem', and, in the first issue of the local newspaper after the death, to explain without offence that Silas had taken 'a day off'. It was more than a day, but from the record it appears that well within a month Mr Deemer made it plain that he had not the leisure to be dead.

One of Hillbrook's most respected citizens was Alvan Creede, a banker. He lived in the finest house in town, kept a carriage and was a most estimable man variously. He knew something of the advantages of travel, too, having been frequently in Boston, and once, it was thought, in New York, though he modestly disclaimed that glittering distinction. The matter is mentioned here merely as a contribution to an understanding of Mr Creede's worth, for either way it is creditable to him – to his intelligence if he had put himself, even temporarily, into contact with metropolitan culture; to his candour if he had not.

One pleasant summer evening at about the hour of ten Mr Creede, entering at his garden gate, passed up the gravel walk, which looked very white in the moonlight, mounted the stone steps of his fine house and pausing a moment inserted his latchkey in the door. As he pushed this open he met his wife, who was crossing the passage from the parlour to the library. She greeted him pleasantly and pulling the door farther back held it for him to enter. Instead he turned and, looking about his feet in front of the threshold, uttered an exclamation of surprise.

'Why! – what the devil,' he said, 'has become of that jug?'

'What jug, Alvan?' his wife inquired, not very sympathetically.

'A jug of maple syrup – I brought it along from the store and set it down here to open the door. What the – '

'There, there, Alvan, please don't swear again,' said the lady, interrupting. Hillbrook, by the way, is not the only place in Christendom where a vestigial polytheism forbids the taking in vain of the Evil One's name.

The jug of maple syrup which the easy ways of village life had permitted Hillbrook's foremost citizen to carry home from the store was not there.

'Are you quite sure, Alvan?'

'My dear, do you suppose a man does not know when he is carrying a jug? I bought that syrup at Deemer's as I was passing. Deemer himself drew it and lent me the jug, and I – '

The sentence remains to this day unfinished. Mr Creede staggered into the house, entered the parlour and dropped into an armchair, trembling in every limb. He had suddenly remembered that Silas Deemer was three weeks dead.

Mrs Creede stood by her husband, regarding him with surprise and anxiety.

'For Heaven's sake,' she said, 'what ails you?'

Mr Creede's ailment having no obvious relation to the interests of the better land he did not apparently deem it necessary to expound it on that demand; he said nothing – merely stared. There were long moments of silence broken by nothing but the measured ticking of the clock, which seemed somewhat slower than usual, as if it were civilly granting them an extension of time in which to recover their wits.

'Jane, I have gone mad – that is it.' He spoke thickly and hurriedly. 'You should have told me; you must have observed my symptoms before they became so pronounced that I have observed them myself. I thought I was passing Deemer's store; it was open and lit up – that is what I thought; of course it is never open now. Silas Deemer stood at his desk behind the counter. My God, Jane, I saw him as distinctly as I see you. Remembering that you had said you wanted some maple syrup, I went in and bought some – that is all – I bought two quarts of maple syrup from Silas Deemer, who is dead and underground, but nevertheless drew that syrup from a cask and handed it to me in a jug. He talked with me, too, rather gravely, I remember, even more so than was his way, but not a word of what he said can I now recall. But I saw him – good Lord, I saw and talked with him – and he is dead! So I thought, but I'm mad, Jane, I'm as crazy as a beetle; and you have kept it from me.'

This monologue gave the woman time to collect what faculties she had.

'Alvan,' she said, 'you have given no evidence of insanity, believe me. This was undoubtedly an illusion – how should it be anything else? That would be too terrible! But there is no insanity; you are working too hard at the bank. You should not have attended the meeting of directors this evening; anyone could see that you were ill; I knew something would occur.'

It may have seemed to him that the prophecy had lagged a bit, awaiting the event, but he said nothing of that, being concerned with his own condition. He was calm now, and could think coherently.

'Doubtless the phenomenon was subjective,' he said, with a some-what ludicrous transition to the slang of science. 'Granting the possibility of spiritual apparition and even materialisation, yet the apparition and materialisation of a half-gallon brown clay jug – a piece of coarse, heavy pottery evolved from nothing – that is hardly thinkable.'

As he finished speaking, a child ran into the room – his little daughter. She was clad in a bedgown. Hastening to her father she threw her arms about his neck, saying: 'You naughty papa, you forgot to come in and kiss me. We heard you open the gate and got up and looked out. And, papa dear, Eddy says mayn't he have the little jug when it is empty?'

As the full import of that revelation imparted itself to Alvan Creede's understanding he visibly shuddered. For the child could not have heard a word of the conversation.

The estate of Silas Deemer being in the hands of an administrator who had thought it best to dispose of the 'business', the store had been closed ever since the owner's death, the goods having been removed by another 'merchant' who had purchased them *en bloc*. The rooms above were vacant as well, for the widow and daughters had gone to another town.

On the evening immediately after Alvan Creede's adventure (which had somehow 'got out') a crowd of men, women and children thronged the sidewalk opposite the store. That the place was haunted by the spirit of the late Silas Deemer was now well known to every resident of Hillbrook, though many affected disbelief. Of these the hardiest, and in a general way the youngest, threw stones against the front of the building, the only part accessible, but carefully missed the unshuttered windows. Incredulity had not grown to malice. A few venturesome souls crossed the street and rattled the door in its frame; struck matches and held them near the window; attempted to view the black interior. Some of the spectators invited attention to their wit by shouting and groaning and challenging the ghost to a foot-race.

After a considerable time had elapsed without any manifestation, and many of the crowd had gone away, all those remaining began to observe that the interior of the store was suffused with a dim, yellow light. At this all demonstrations ceased; the intrepid souls about the door and windows fell back to the opposite side of the street and were merged in the crowd; the small boys ceased throwing stones. Nobody spoke above his breath; all whispered excitedly and pointed to the now steadily growing light. How long a time had passed since the first faint glow had been observed none could have guessed, but eventually the illumination was bright enough to reveal the whole interior of the store; and there, standing at his desk behind the counter Silas Deemer was distinctly visible!

The effect upon the crowd was marvellous. It began rapidly to melt away at both flanks, as the timid left the place. Many ran as fast as their legs would let them; others moved off with greater dignity, turning occasionally to look backward over the shoulder. At last a score or more, mostly men, remained where they were, speechless, staring, excited. The apparition inside gave them no attention; it was apparently occupied with a book of accounts.

Presently three men left the crowd on the sidewalk as if by a common impulse and crossed the street. One of them, a heavy man, was about to set his shoulder against the door when it opened, apparently without human agency, and the courageous investigators passed in. No sooner had they crossed the threshold than they were seen by the awed observers outside to be acting in the most unaccountable way. They thrust out their hands before them, pursued devious courses, came into violent collision with the counter, with boxes and barrels on the floor, and with one another. They turned awkwardly hither and thither and seemed trying to escape, but unable to retrace their steps. Their voices were heard in exclamations and curses. But in no way did the apparition of Silas Deemer manifest an interest in what was going on.

By what impulse the crowd was moved none ever recollected, but the entire mass – men, women, children, dogs – made a simultaneous and tumultuous rush for the entrance. They congested the doorway, pushing for precedence – resolving themselves at length into a line and moving up step by step. By some subtle spiritual or physical alchemy observation had been transmuted into action – the sightseers had become participants in the spectacle – the audience had usurped the stage.

To the only spectator remaining on the other side of the street – Alvan Creede, the banker – the interior of the store with its inpouring crowd continued in full illumination; all the strange things going on there were clearly visible. To those inside all was black darkness. It was as if each person as he was thrust in at the door had been stricken blind, and was maddened by the mischance. They groped with aimless imprecision, tried to force their way out against the current, pushed and elbowed, struck at random, fell and were trampled, rose and trampled in their turn. They seized one another by the garments, the hair, the beard – fought like animals, cursed, shouted, called one another opprobrious and obscene names. When, finally, Alvan Creede had seen the last person of the line pass into that awful tumult the light that had illuminated it was suddenly quenched and all was as black to him as to those within. He turned away and left he place.

In the early morning a curious crowd had gathered about 'Deemer's'. It was composed partly of those who had run away the night before, but now had the courage of sunshine, partly of honest folk going to their daily toil. The door of the store stood open; the place was vacant, but on the walls, the floor, the furniture, were shreds of clothing and tangles of hair. Hillbrook militant had managed somehow to pull itself out and had gone home to medicine its hurts and swear that it had been all night in bed. On the dusty desk, behind the counter, was the sales book. The entries in it, in Deemer's handwriting, had ceased on the 16th day of July, the last of his life. There was no record of a later sale to Alvan Creede.

That is the entire story – except that men's passions having subsided and reason having resumed its immemorial sway, it was confessed in Hillbrook that, considering the harmless and honourable character of his first commercial transaction under the new conditions, Silas Deemer, deceased, might properly have been suffered to resume business at the old stand without mobbing. In that judgement the local historian from whose unpublished work these facts are compiled had the thoughtfulness to signify his concurrence.

Staley Flaming's Hallucination

Of two men who were talking one was a physician.

'I sent for you, doctor,' said the other, 'but I don't think you can do me any good. Maybe you can recommend a specialist in psychopathy. I fancy I'm a bit loony.'

'You look all right,' the physician said.

'You shall judge – I have hallucinations. I wake every night and see in my room, intently watching me, a big black Newfoundland dog with a white forefoot.'

'You say you wake; are you sure about that? "Hallucinations" are sometimes only dreams.'

'Oh, I wake all right. Sometimes I lie still a long time, looking at the dog as earnestly as the dog looks at me – I always leave the light going. When I can't endure it any longer I sit up in bed – and nothing is there!'

' 'M, 'm – what is the beast's expression?'

'It seems to me sinister. Of course I know that, except in art, an animal's face in repose has always the same expression. But this is not a real animal. Newfoundland dogs are pretty mild looking, you know; what's the matter with this one?'

'Really, my diagnosis would have no value: I am not going to treat the dog.'

The physician laughed at his own pleasantry, but narrowly watched his patient from the corner of his eye. Presently he said: 'Fleming, your description of the beast fits the dog of the late Atwell Barton.'

Fleming half rose from his chair, sat again and made a visible attempt at indifference. 'I remember Barton,' he said; 'I believe he was – it was reported that – wasn't there something suspicious in his death?'

Looking squarely now into the eyes of his patient, the physician said: 'Three years ago the body of your old enemy, Atwell Barton, was found in the woods near his house and yours. He had been stabbed to death. There have been no arrests; there was no clue. Some of us had "theories". I had one. Have you?'

'I? Why, bless your soul, what could I know about it? You remember that I left for Europe almost immediately afterward – a considerable time afterward. In the few weeks since my return you could not expect me to construct a "theory". In fact, I have not given the matter a thought. What about his dog?'

'It was first to find the body. It died of starvation on his grave.'

We do not know the inexorable law underlying coincidences. Staley Fleming did not, or he would perhaps not have sprung to his feet as the night wind brought in through the open window the long wailing howl of a distant dog. He strode several times across the room in the steadfast gaze of the physician; then, abruptly confronting him, almost shouted: 'What has all this to do with my trouble, Dr Halderman? You forget why you were sent for.'

Rising, the physician laid his hand upon his patient's arm and said, gently: 'Pardon me. I cannot diagnose your disorder offhand – tomorrow, perhaps. Please go to bed, leaving your door unlocked; I will pass the night here with your books. Can you call me without rising?'

'Yes, there is an electric bell.'

'Good. If anything disturbs you push the button without sitting up. Good-night.'

Comfortably installed in an armchair the man of medicine stared into the glowing coals and thought deeply and long, but apparently to little purpose, for he frequently rose and opening a door leading to the staircase, listened intently; then resumed his seat. Presently, however, he fell asleep, and when he woke it was past midnight. He stirred the failing fire, lifted a book from the table at his side and looked at the title. It was Denneker's *Meditations*. He opened it at random and began to read:

Forasmuch as it is ordained of God that all flesh hath spirit and thereby taketh on spiritual powers, so, also, the spirit hath powers of the flesh, even when it is gone out of the flesh and liveth as a thing apart, as many a violence performed by wraith and lemure sheweth. And there be who say that man is not single in this, but the beasts have the like evil inducement, and –

The reading was interrupted by a shaking of the house, as by the fall of a heavy object. The reader flung down the book, rushed from the room and mounted the stairs to Fleming's bedchamber. He tried the door, but contrary to his instructions it was locked. He set his shoulder against it with such force that it gave way. On the floor near the disordered bed, in his night-clothes, lay Fleming, gasping away his life.

The physician raised the dying man's head from the floor and observed a wound in the throat. 'I should have thought of this,' he said, believing it suicide.

When the man was dead an examination disclosed the unmistakable marks of an animal's fangs deeply sunken into the jugular vein.

But there was no animal.

A Resumed Identity

The Review as a form of Welcome

One summer night a man stood on a low hill overlooking a wide expanse of forest and field. By the full moon hanging low in the west he knew what he might not have known otherwise: that it was near the hour of dawn. A light mist lay along the earth, partly veiling the lower features of the landscape, but above it the taller trees showed in well-defined masses against a clear sky. Two or three farmhouses were visible through the haze, but in none of them, naturally, was a light. Nowhere, indeed, was any sign or suggestion of life except the barking of a distant dog, which, repeated with mechanical iteration, served rather to accentuate than dispel the loneliness of the scene.

The man looked curiously about him on all sides, as one who among familiar surroundings is unable to determine his exact place and part in the scheme of things. It is so, perhaps, that we shall act when, risen from the dead, we await the call to judgement.

A hundred yards away was a straight road, showing white in the moonlight. Endeavouring to orient himself, as a surveyor or navigator might say, the man moved his eyes slowly along its visible length and at a distance of a quarter-mile to the south of his station saw, dim and grey in the haze, a group of horsemen riding to the north. Behind them were men afoot, marching in column, with dimly gleaming rifles aslant above their shoulders. They moved slowly and in silence. Another group of horsemen, another regiment of infantry, another and another – all in unceasing motion toward the man's point of view, past it, and beyond. A battery of artillery followed, the cannoneers riding with folded arms on limber and caisson. And still the interminable procession came out of the obscurity to south and passed into the obscurity to north, with never a sound of voice, nor hoof, nor wheel.

The man could not rightly understand: he thought himself deaf; said so, and heard his own voice, although it had an unfamiliar quality – that almost alarmed him; it disappointed his ear's expectancy in the matter of timbre and resonance. But he was not deaf, and that for the moment sufficed.

Then he remembered that there are natural phenomena to which someone has given the name 'acoustic shadows'. If you stand in an acoustic shadow there is one direction from which you will hear nothing. At the battle of Gaines's Mill, one of the fiercest conflicts of the Civil War, with a hundred guns in play, spectators a mile and a half away on the opposite side of the Chickahominy valley heard nothing of what they clearly saw. The bombardment of Port Royal, heard and felt at St Augustine, a hundred and fifty miles to the south, was inaudible two miles to the north in a still atmosphere. A few days before the surrender at Appomattox a thunderous engagement between the commands of Sheridan and Pickett was unknown to the latter commander, a mile in the rear of his own line.

These instances were not known to the man of whom we write, but less striking ones of the same character had not escaped his observation. He was profoundly disquieted, but for another reason than the uncanny silence of that moonlight march.

'Good Lord!' he said to himself – and again it was as if another had spoken his thought – 'if those people are what I take them to be we have lost the battle and they are moving on Nashville!'

Then came a thought of self – an apprehension – a strong sense of personal peril, such as in another we call fear. He stepped quickly into the shadow of a tree. And still the silent battalions moved slowly forward in the haze.

The chill of a sudden breeze upon the back of his neck drew his attention to the quarter whence it came, and turning to the east he saw a faint grey light along the horizon – the first sign of returning day. This increased his apprehension.

'I must get away from here,' he thought, 'or I shall be discovered and taken.'

He moved out of the shadow, walking rapidly toward the greying east. From the safer seclusion of a clump of cedars he looked back. The entire column had passed out of sight: the straight white road lay bare and desolate in the moonlight!

Puzzled before, he was now inexpressibly astonished. So swift a passing of so slow an army! – he could not comprehend it. Minute after minute passed unnoted; he had lost his sense of time. He sought with a terrible earnestness a solution of the mystery, but sought in vain. When at last he roused himself from his abstraction the sun's rim was visible above the hills, but in the new conditions he found no other light than that of day; his understanding was involved as darkly in doubt as before.

On every side lay cultivated fields showing no sign of war and war's ravages. From the chimneys of the farmhouses thin ascensions of blue smoke signalled preparations for a day's peaceful toil. Having stilled its immemorial allocution to the moon, the watch-dog was assisting a negro who, prefixing a team of mules to the plough, was flatting and sharping contentedly at his task. The hero of this tale stared stupidly at the pastoral picture as if he had never seen such a thing in all his life; then he put his hand to his head, passed it through his hair and, withdrawing it, attentively considered the palm – a singular thing to do. Apparently reassured by the act, he walked confidently toward the road.

❦ TWO ❧

When you have lost your Life consult a Physician

Dr Stilling Malson, of Murfreesboro, having visited a patient six or seven miles away, on the Nashville road, had remained with him all night. At daybreak he set out for home on horseback, as was the custom of doctors of the time and region. He had passed into the neighbour-hood of Stone's River battlefield when a man approached him from the roadside and saluted in the military fashion, with a movement of the right hand to the hat-brim. But the hat was not a military hat, the man was not in uniform and had not a martial bearing. The doctor nodded civilly, half thinking that the stranger's uncommon greeting was perhaps in deference to the historic surroundings. As the stranger evidently desired speech with him he courteously reined in his horse and waited.

'Sir,' said the stranger, 'although a civilian, you are perhaps an enemy.'

'I am a physician,' was the non-committal reply.

'Thank you,' said the other. 'I am a lieutenant, of the staff of General Hazen.' He paused a moment and looked sharply at the person whom he was addressing, then added, 'Of the Federal army.'

The physician merely nodded.

'Kindly tell me,' continued the other, 'what has happened here. Where are the armies? Which has won the battle?'

The physician regarded his questioner curiously with half-shut eyes. After a professional scrutiny, prolonged to the limit of politeness, 'Pardon me,' he said; 'one asking information should be willing to impart it. Are you wounded?' he added, smiling.

'Not seriously – it seems.'

The man removed the unmilitary hat, put his hand to his head, passed it through his hair and, withdrawing it, attentively considered the palm.

'I was struck by a bullet and have been unconscious. It must have been a light, glancing blow: I find no blood and feel no pain. I will not trouble you for treatment, but will you kindly direct me to my command to any part of the Federal army – if you know?'

Again the doctor did not immediately reply: he was recalling much that is recorded in the books of his profession – something about lost identity and the effect of familiar scenes in restoring it. At length he looked the man in the face, smiled, and said: 'Lieutenant, you are not wearing the uniform of your rank and service.'

At this the man glanced down at his civilian attire, lifted his eyes, and said with hesitation:

'That is true. I – I don't quite understand.'

Still regarding him sharply but not unsympathetically, the man of science bluntly inquired: 'How old are you?'

'Twenty-three – if that has anything to do with it.'

'You don't look it; I should hardly have guessed you to be just that.'

The man was growing impatient. 'We need not discuss that,' he said; 'I want to know about the army. Not two hours ago I saw a column of troops moving northward on this road. You must have met them. Be good enough to tell me the colour of their clothing, which I was unable to make out, and I'll trouble you no more.'

'You are quite sure that you saw them?'

'Sure? My God, sir, I could have counted them!'

'Why, really,' said the physician, with an amusing consciousness of his own resemblance to the loquacious barber of the *Arabian Nights*, 'this is very interesting. I met no troops.'

The man looked at him coldly, as if he had himself observed the likeness to the barber. 'It is plain,' he said, 'that you do not care to assist me. Sir, you may go to the devil!'

He turned and strode away, very much at random, across the dewy fields, his half-penitent tormentor quietly watching him from his point of vantage in the saddle till he disappeared beyond an array of trees.

❧ THREE ❧

The Danger of looking into a Pool of Water

After leaving the road the man slackened his pace, and now went forward, rather deviously, with a distinct feeling of fatigue. He could not account for this, though truly the interminable loquacity of that country doctor offered itself in explanation. Seating himself upon a rock, he laid one hand upon his knee, back upward, and casually looked at it. It was lean and withered. He lifted both hands to his face. It was seamed and furrowed; he could trace the lines with the tips of his fingers. How strange! – a mere bullet-stroke and a brief unconsciousness should not make one a physical wreck.

'I must have been a long time in hospital,' he said aloud. 'Why, what a fool I am! The battle was in December, and it is now summer!' He laughed. 'No wonder that fellow thought me an escaped lunatic. He was wrong: I am only an escaped patient.'

At a little distance a small plot of ground enclosed by a stone wall caught his attention. With no very definite intent he rose and went to it. In the centre was a square, solid monument of hewn stone. It was brown with age, weather-worn at the angles, spotted with moss and lichen. Between the massive blocks were strips of grass the leverage of whose roots had pushed them apart. In answer to the challenge of this ambitious structure Time had laid his destroying hand upon it, and it would soon be 'one with Nineveh and Tyre'. In an inscription on one side his eye caught a familiar name. Shaking with excitement, he craned his body across the wall and read:

HAZEN'S BRIGADE
TO
THE MEMORY OF ITS SOLDIERS
WHO FELL AT
STONE RIVER, 31 DECEMBER 1862

The man fell back from the wall, faint and sick. Almost within an arm's length was a little depression in the earth; it had been filled by a recent rain – a pool of clear water. He crept to it to revive himself, lifted the upper part of his body on his trembling arms, thrust forward his head and saw the reflection of his face, as in a mirror. He uttered a terrible cry. His arms gave way; he fell, face downward, into the pool and yielded up the life that had spanned another life.

A Baby Tramp

If you had seen little Jo standing at the street corner in the rain, you would hardly have admired him. It was apparently an ordinary autumn rainstorm, but the water which fell upon Jo (who was hardly old enough to be either just or unjust, and so perhaps did not come under the law of impartial distribution) appeared to have some property peculiar to itself: one would have said it was dark and adhesive – sticky. But that could hardly be so, even in Blackburg, where things certainly did occur that were a good deal out of the common.

For example, ten or twelve years before, a shower of small frogs had fallen, as is credibly attested by a contemporaneous chronicle, the record concluding with a somewhat obscure statement to the effect that the chronicler considered it good growing-weather for Frenchmen.

Some years later Blackburg had a fall of crimson snow; it is cold in Blackburg when winter is on, and the snows are frequent and deep. There can be no doubt of it – the snow in this instance was of the colour of blood and melted into water of the same hue, if water it was, not blood. The phenomenon had attracted wide attention, and science had as many explanations as there were scientists who knew nothing about it. But the men of Blackburg – men who for many years had lived right there where the red snow fell, and might be supposed to know a good deal about the matter – shook their heads and said something would come of it.

And something did, for the next summer was made memorable by the prevalence of a mysterious disease epidemic, endemic, or the Lord knows what, though the physicians didn't – which carried away a full half of the population. Most of the other half carried themselves away and were slow to return, but finally came back, and were now increasing and multiplying as before, but Blackburg had not since been altogether the same.

Of quite another kind, though equally 'out of the common', was the incident of Hetty Parlow's ghost. Hetty Parlow's maiden name had been

Brownon, and in Blackburg that meant more than one would think.

The Brownons had from time immemorial – from the very earliest of the old colonial days – been the leading family of the town. It was the richest and it was the best, and Blackburg would have shed the last drop of its plebeian blood in defence of the Brownon fair fame. As few of the family's members had ever been known to live permanently away from Blackburg, although most of them were educated elsewhere and nearly all had travelled, there was quite a number of them. The men held most of the public offices, and the women were foremost in all good works. Of these latter, Hetty was most beloved by reason of the sweetness of her disposition, the purity of her character and her singular personal beauty. She married in Boston a young scapegrace named Parlow, and like a good Brownon brought him to Blackburg forthwith and made a man and a town councillor of him. They had a child which they named Joseph and dearly loved, as was then the fashion among parents in all that region. Then they died of the mysterious disorder already mentioned, and at the age of one whole year Joseph set up as an orphan.

Unfortunately for Joseph the disease which had cut off his parents did not stop at that; it went on and extirpated nearly the whole Brownon contingent and its allies by marriage; and those who fled did not return. The tradition was broken, the Brownon estates passed into alien hands, and the only Brownons remaining in that place were underground in Oak Hill Cemetery, where, indeed, was a colony of them powerful enough to resist the encroachment of surrounding tribes and hold the best part of the grounds. But about the ghost:

One night, about three years after the death of Hetty Parlow, a number of the young people of Blackburg were passing Oak Hill Cemetery in a wagon – if you have been there you will remember that the road to Greenton runs alongside it on the south. They had been attending a May Day festival at Greenton; and that serves to fix the date. Altogether there may have been a dozen, and a jolly party they were, considering the legacy of gloom left by the town's recent sombre experiences. As they passed the cemetery the man driving suddenly reined in his team with an exclamation of surprise. It was sufficiently surprising, no doubt, for just ahead, and almost at the roadside, though inside the cemetery, stood the ghost of Hetty Parlow. There could be no doubt of it, for she had been personally known to every youth and maiden in the party. That established the thing's identity; its character as ghost was signified by all the customary signs – the shroud, the long, undone hair, the 'far-away look' – everything. This disquieting apparition was stretching out its arms toward the west, as if in supplication for the evening star, which, certainly, was an alluring object, though obviously out of reach. As they all sat silent (so the story goes) every member of that party of merrymakers – they had merrymade on coffee and lemonade only – distinctly heard that ghost call the name 'Joey, Joey!' A moment later nothing was there. Of course one does not have to believe all that.

Now, at that moment, as was afterward ascertained, Joey was wandering about in the sagebrush on the opposite side of the continent, near Winnemucca, in the State of Nevada. He had been taken to that town by some good persons distantly related to his dead father, and by them adopted and tenderly cared for. But on that evening the poor child had strayed from home and was lost in the desert.

His after history is involved in obscurity and has gaps which conjecture alone can fill. It is known that he was found by a family of Piute Indians, who kept the little wretch with them for a time and then sold him – actually sold him for money to a woman on one of the eastbound trains, at a station a long way from Winnemucca. The woman professed to have made all manner of inquiries, but all in vain: so, being childless and a widow, she adopted him herself. At this point of his career Jo seemed to be getting a long way from the condition of orphanage; the interposition of a multitude of parents between himself and that woeful state promised him a long immunity from its disadvantages.

Mrs Darnell, his newest mother, lived in Cleveland, Ohio. But her adopted son did not long remain with her. He was seen one afternoon by a policeman, new to that beat, deliberately toddling away from her house, and being questioned answered that he was 'a doin' home.' He must have travelled by rail, somehow, for three days later he was in the town of Whiteville, which, as you know, is a long way from Blackburg. His clothing was in pretty fair condition, but he was sinfully dirty. Unable to give any account of himself he was arrested as a vagrant and sentenced to imprisonment in the Infants' Sheltering Home – where he was washed.

Jo ran away from the Infants' Sheltering Home at Whiteville – just took to the woods one day, and the Home knew him no more for ever.

We find him next, or rather get back to him, standing forlorn in the cold autumn rain at a suburban street corner in Blackburg; and it seems right to explain now that the raindrops falling upon him there were really not dark and gummy; they only failed to make his face and hands less so. Jo was indeed fearfully and wonderfully besmirched, as by the hand of an artist. And the forlorn little tramp had no shoes; his feet were bare, red, and swollen, and when he walked he limped with both legs. As to clothing – ah, you would hardly have had the skill to name any single garment that he wore, or say by what magic he kept it upon him. That he was cold all over and all through did not admit of a doubt; he knew it himself. Anyone would have been cold there that evening; but, for that reason, no one else was there. How Jo came to be there himself, he could not for the flickering little life of him have told, even if gifted with a vocabulary exceeding a hundred words. From the way he stared about him one could have seen that he had not the faintest notion of where (nor why) he was.

Yet he was not altogether a fool in his day and generation; being cold and hungry, and still able to walk a little by bending his knees very much indeed and putting his feet down toes first, he decided to enter one of the houses which flanked the street at long intervals and looked so bright and warm. But when he attempted to act upon that very sensible decision a burly dog came browsing out and disputed his right. Inexpressibly frightened, and believing, no doubt (with some reason, too), that brutes without meant brutality within, he hobbled away from all the houses, and with grey, wet fields to right of him and grey, wet fields to left of him – with the rain half blinding him and the night coming in mist and darkness, held his way along the road that leads to Greenton. That is to say, the road leads those to Greenton who succeed in passing the Oak Hill Cemetery. A considerable number every year do not.

Jo did not.

They found him there the next morning, very wet, very cold, but no longer hungry. He had apparently entered the cemetery gate – hoping, perhaps, that it led to a house where there was no dog – and gone blundering about in the darkness, falling over many a grave, no doubt, until he had tired of it all and given up. The little body lay upon one side, with one soiled cheek upon one soiled hand, the other hand tucked away among the rags to make it warm, the other cheek washed clean and white at last, as for a kiss from one of God's great angels. It was observed – though nothing was thought of it at the time, the body being as yet unidentified – that the little fellow was lying upon the grave of Hetty Parlow. The grave, however, had not opened to receive him. That is a circumstance which, without actual irreverence, one may wish had been ordered otherwise.

The Night-Doings at Deadman's

A Story that is Untrue

It was a singularly sharp night, and clear as the heart of a diamond. Clear nights have a trick of being keen. In darkness you may be cold and not know it; when you see, you suffer. This night was bright enough to bite like a serpent. The moon was moving mysteriously along behind the giant pines crowning the South Mountain, striking a cold sparkle from the crusted snow, and bringing out against the black west and ghostly outlines of the Coast Range, beyond which lay the invisible Pacific. The snow had piled itself, in the open spaces along the bottom of the gulch, into long ridges that seemed to heave, and into hills that appeared to toss and scatter spray. The spray was sunlight, twice reflected: dashed once from the moon, once from the snow.

In this snow many of the shanties of the abandoned mining camp were obliterated (a sailor might have said they had gone down), and at irregular intervals it had overtopped the tall trestles which had once supported a river called a flume; for, of course, 'flume' is *flumen*. Among the advantages of which the mountains cannot deprive the gold-hunter is the privilege of speaking Latin. He says of his dead neighbour, 'He has gone up the flume.' This is not a bad way to say, 'His life has returned to the Fountain of Life.'

While putting on its armour against the assaults of the wind, this snow had neglected no coign of vantage. Snow pursued by the wind is not wholly unlike a retreating army. In the open field it ranges itself in ranks and battalions; where it can get a foothold it makes a stand; where it can take cover it does so. You may see whole platoons of snow cowering behind a bit of broken wall. The devious old road, hewn out of the mountainside, was full of it. Squadron upon squadron had struggled to escape by this line, when suddenly pursuit had ceased. A more desolate and dreary spot than Deadman's Gulch in a winter midnight it is impossible to imagine. Yet Mr Hiram Beeson elected to live there, the sole inhabitant.

Away up the side of the North Mountain his little pine-log shanty projected from its single pane of glass a long, thin beam of light, and looked not altogether unlike a black beetle fastened to the hillside with a bright new pin. Within it sat Mr Beeson himself, before a roaring fire, staring into its hot heart as if he had never before seen such a thing in all his life. He was not a comely man. He was grey; he was ragged and slovenly in his attire; his face was wan and haggard; his eyes were too bright. As to his age, if one had attempted to guess it, one might have said forty-seven, then corrected himself and said seventy-four. He was really twenty-eight. Emaciated he was; as much, perhaps, as he dared be, with a needy undertaker at Bentley's Flat and a new and enterprising coroner at Sonora. Poverty and zeal are an upper and a nether millstone. It is dangerous to make a third in that kind of sandwich.

As Mr Beeson sat there, with his ragged elbows on his ragged knees, his lean jaws buried in his lean hands, and with no apparent intention of going to bed, he looked as if the slightest movement would tumble him to pieces. Yet during the last hour he had winked no fewer than three times.

There was a sharp rapping at the door. A rap at that time of night and in that weather might have surprised an ordinary mortal who had dwelt two years in the gulch without seeing a human face, and could not fail to know that the country was impassable; but Mr Beeson did not so much as pull his eyes out of the coals. And even when the door was pushed open he only shrugged a little more closely into himself, as one does who is expecting something that he would rather not see. You may observe this movement in women when, in a mortuary chapel, the coffin is borne up the aisle behind them.

But when a long old man in a blanket overcoat, his head tied up in a handkerchief and nearly his entire face in a muffler, wearing green goggles and with a complexion of glittering whiteness where it could be seen, strode silently into the room, laying a hard, gloved hand on Mr Beeson's shoulder, the latter so far forgot himself as to look up with an appearance of no small astonishment; whomever he may have been expecting, he had evidently not counted on meeting anyone like this. Nevertheless, the sight of this unexpected guest produced in Mr Beeson the following sequence: a feeling of astonishment; a sense of gratification; a sentiment of profound good will. Rising from his seat, he took the knotty hand from his shoulder, and shook it up and down with a fervour quite unaccountable; for in the old man's aspect was nothing to attract, much to repel. However, attraction is too general a property for repulsion to be without it. The most attractive object in the world is the face we instinctively cover with a cloth. When it becomes still more attractive – fascinating – we put seven feet of earth above it.

'Sir,' said Mr Beeson, releasing the old man's hand, which fell passively against his thigh with a quiet clack, 'it is an extremely disagreeable night. Pray be seated; I am very glad to see you.'

Mr Beeson spoke with an easy good breeding that one would hardly have expected, considering all things. Indeed, the contrast between his appearance and his manner was sufficiently surprising to be one of the commonest of social phenomena in the mines. The old man advanced a step toward the fire, glowing cavernously in the green goggles.

Mr Beeson resumed: 'You bet your life I am!'

Mr Beeson's elegance was not too refined; it had made reasonable concessions to local taste. He paused a moment, letting his eyes drop from the muffled head of his guest, down along the row of mouldy buttons confining the blanket overcoat, to the greenish cowhide boots powdered with snow, which had begun to melt and run along the floor in little rills. He took an inventory of his guest, and appeared satisfied. Who would not have been? Then he continued: 'The cheer I can offer you is, unfortunately, in keeping with my surroundings; but I shall esteem myself highly favoured if it is your pleasure to partake of it, rather than seek better at Bentley's Flat.'

With a singular refinement of hospitable humility Mr Beeson spoke as if a sojourn in his warm cabin on such a night, as compared with walking fourteen miles up to the throat in snow with a cutting crust, would be an intolerable hardship. By way of reply, his guest unbuttoned the blanket overcoat. The host laid fresh fuel on the fire, swept the hearth with the tail of a wolf, and added: 'But *I* think you'd better skedaddle.'

The old man took a seat by the fire, spreading his broad soles to the heat without removing his hat. In the mines the hat is seldom removed except when the boots are. Without further remark Mr Beeson also seated himself in a chair which had been a barrel, and which, retaining much of its original character, seemed to have been designed with a view to preserving his dust if it should please him to crumble. For a moment there was silence; then, from somewhere among the pines, came the snarling yelp of a coyote; and simultaneously the door rattled in its frame. There was no other connection between the two incidents than that the coyote has an aversion to storms, and the wind was rising; yet there seemed somehow a kind of supernatural conspiracy between the two, and Mr Beeson shuddered with a vague sense of terror. He recovered himself in a moment and again addressed his guest.

'There are strange doings here. I will tell you everything, and then if you decide to go I shall hope to accompany you over the worst of the way; as far as where Baldy Peterson shot Ben Hike – I dare say you know the place.'

The old man nodded emphatically, as intimating not merely that he did, but that he did indeed.

'Two years ago,' began Mr Beeson, 'I, with two companions, occupied this house; but when the rush to the Flat occurred we left, along with the rest. In ten hours the Gulch was deserted. That evening, however, I discovered I had left behind me a valuable pistol (that is it) and returned for it, passing the night here alone, as I have passed every night since. I must explain that a few days before we left, our Chinese domestic had the misfortune to die while the ground was frozen so hard that it was impossible to dig a grave in the usual way. So, on the day of our hasty departure, we cut through the floor there, and gave him such burial as we could. But before putting him down I had the extremely bad taste to cut off his pigtail and spike it to that beam above his grave, where you may see it at this moment, or, preferably, when warmth has given you leisure for observation.

'I stated, did I not, that the Chinaman came to his death from natural causes? I had, of course, nothing to do with that, and returned through no irresistible attraction, or morbid fascination, but only because I had forgotten a pistol. That is clear to you, is it not, sir?'

The visitor nodded gravely. He appeared to be a man of few words, if any.

Mr Beeson continued: 'According to the Chinese faith, a man is like a kite: he cannot go to heaven without a tail. Well, to shorten this tedious story – which, however, I thought it my duty to relate – on that night, while I was here alone and thinking of anything but him, that Chinaman came back for his pigtail.

'He did not get it.'

At this point Mr Beeson relapsed into blank silence. Perhaps he was fatigued by the unwonted exercise of speaking; perhaps he had conjured up a memory that demanded his undivided attention. The wind was now fairly abroad, and the pines along the mountainside sang with singular distinctness.

The narrator continued: 'You say you do not see much in that, and I must confess I do not myself.

'But he keeps coming!'

There was another long silence, during which both stared into the fire without the movement of a limb. Then Mr Beeson broke out, almost fiercely, fixing his eyes on what he could see of the impassive face of his auditor: 'Give it him? Sir, in this matter I have no intention of troubling anyone for advice. You will pardon me, I am sure' – here he became singularly persuasive – 'but I have ventured to nail that pigtail fast, and have assumed the somewhat onerous obligation of guarding it. So it is quite impossible to act on your considerate suggestion.

'Do you play me for a Modoc?'

Nothing could exceed the sudden ferocity with which he thrust this indignant remonstrance into the ear of his guest. It was as if he had struck him on the side of the head with a steel gauntlet. It was a protest, but it was a challenge. To be mistaken for a coward – to be played for a Modoc: these two expressions are one. Sometimes it is a Chinaman. Do you play me for a Chinaman? is a question frequently addressed to the ear of the suddenly dead.

Mr Beeson's buffet produced no effect, and after a moment's pause, during which the wind thundered in the chimney like the sound of clods upon a coffin, he resumed: 'But, as you say, it is wearing me out. I feel that the life of the last two years has been a mistake – a mistake that corrects itself; you see how. The grave! No; there is no one to dig it. The ground is frozen, too. But you are very welcome. You may say at Bentley's – but that is not important. It was very tough to cut; they braid silk into their pigtails. Kwaagh.'

Mr Beeson was speaking with his eyes shut, and he wandered. His last word was a snore. A moment later he drew a long breath, opened his eyes with an effort, made a single remark, and fell into a deep sleep. What he said was this: 'They are swiping my dust!'

Then the aged stranger, who had not uttered one word since his arrival, arose from his seat and deliberately laid off his outer clothing, looking as angular in his flannels as the late Signorina Festorazzi, an Irish woman, six feet in height, and weighing fifty-six pounds, who used to exhibit herself in her chemise to the people of San Francisco. He then crept into one of the 'bunks', having first placed a revolver in easy reach, according to the custom of the country. This revolver he took from a shelf, and it was the one which Mr Beeson had mentioned as that for which he had returned to the Gulch two years before.

In a few moments Mr Beeson awoke, and seeing that his guest had retired he did likewise. But before doing so he approached the long, plaited wisp of pagan hair and gave it a powerful tug, to assure himself that it was fast and firm. The two beds – mere shelves covered with blankets not overclean – faced each other from opposite sides of the room, the little square trap-door that had given access to the China-man's grave being midway between. This, by the way, was crossed by a double row of spike-heads. In his resistance to the supernatural, Mr Beeson had not disdained the use of material precautions.

The fire was now low, the flames burning bluely and petulantly, with occasional flashes, projecting spectral shadows on the walls – shadows that moved mysteriously about, now dividing, now uniting. The shadow of the pendent queue, however, kept moodily apart, near the roof at the farther end of the room, looking like a note of admiration. The song of the pines outside had now risen to the dignity of a triumphal hymn. In the pauses the silence was dreadful.

It was during one of these intervals that the trap in the floor began to lift. Slowly and steadily it rose, and slowly and steadily rose the swaddled head of the old man in the bunk to observe it. Then, with a clap that shook the house to its foundation, it was thrown clean back, where it lay with its unsightly spikes pointing threateningly upward. Mr Beeson awoke, and without rising, pressed his fingers into his eyes. He shuddered; his teeth chattered. His guest was now reclining on one elbow, watching the proceedings with the goggles that glowed like lamps.

Suddenly a howling gust of wind swooped down the chimney, scattering ashes and smoke in all directions, for a moment obscuring everything. When the firelight again illuminated the room there was seen, sitting gingerly on the edge of a stool by the hearth-side, a swarthy little man of prepossessing appearance and dressed with faultless taste, nodding to the old man with a friendly and engaging smile. 'From San Francisco, evidently,' thought Mr Beeson, who having somewhat recovered from his fright was groping his way to a solution of the evening's events.

But now another actor appeared upon the scene. Out of the square black hole in the middle of the floor protruded the head of the departed Chinaman, his glassy eyes turned upward in their angular slits and fastened on the dangling queue above with a look of yearning unspeakable. Mr Beeson groaned, and again spread his hands upon his face. A mild odour of opium pervaded the place. The phantom, clad only in a short blue tunic quilted and silken but covered with grave-mould, rose slowly, as if pushed by a weak spiral spring. Its knees were at the level of the floor, when with a quick upward impulse like the silent leaping of a flame it grasped the queue with both hands, drew up its body and took the tip in its horrible yellow teeth. To this it clung in a seeming frenzy, grimacing ghastly, surging and plunging from side to side in its efforts to disengage its property from the beam, but uttering no sound. It was like a corpse artificially convulsed by means of a galvanic battery. The contrast between its superhuman activity and its silence was no less than hideous!

Mr Beeson cowered in his bed. The swarthy little gentleman uncrossed his legs, beat an impatient tattoo with the toe of his boot and consulted a heavy gold watch. The old man sat erect and quietly laid hold of the revolver.

Bang!

Like a body cut from the gallows the Chinaman plumped into the black hole below, carrying his tail in his teeth. The trap-door turned over, shutting down with a snap. The swarthy little gentleman from San Francisco sprang nimbly from his perch, caught something in the air with his hat, as a boy catches a butterfly, and vanished into the chimney as if drawn up by suction.

From away somewhere in the outer darkness floated in through the open door a faint, far cry – a long, sobbing wail, as of a child death-strangled in the desert, or a lost soul borne away by the Adversary. It may have been the coyote.

In the early days of the following spring a party of miners on their way to new diggings passed along the Gulch, and straying through the deserted shanties found in one of them the body of Hiram Beeson, stretched upon a bunk, with a bullet hole through the heart. The ball had evidently been fired from the opposite side of the room, for in one of the oaken beams overhead was a shallow blue dint, where it had struck a knot and been deflected downward to the breast of its victim. Strongly attached to the same beam was what appeared to be an end of a rope of braided horsehair, which had been cut by the bullet in its passage to the knot. Nothing else of interest was noted, excepting a suit of mouldy and incongruous clothing, several articles of which were afterward identified by respectable witnesses as those in which certain deceased citizens of Deadman's had been buried years before. But it is not easy to understand how that could be, unless, indeed, the garments had been worn as a disguise by Death himself – which is hardly credible.

Beyond the Wall

Many years ago, on my way from Hong Kong to New York, I passed a week in San Francisco. A long time had gone by since I had been in that city, during which my ventures in the Orient had prospered beyond my hope; I was rich and could afford to revisit my own country to renew my friendship with such of the companions of my youth as still lived and remembered me with the old affection. Chief of these, I hoped, was Mohun Dampier, an old schoolmate with whom I had held a desultory correspondence which had long ceased, as is the way of correspondence between men. You may have observed that the indisposition to write a merely social letter is in the ratio of the square of the distance between you and your correspondent. It is a law.

I remembered Dampier as a handsome, strong young fellow of scholarly tastes, with an aversion to work and a marked indifference to many of the things that the world cares for, including wealth, of which, however, he had inherited enough to put him beyond the reach of want. In his family, one of the oldest and most aristocratic in the country, it was, I think, a matter of pride that no member of it had ever been in trade nor politics, nor suffered any kind of distinction. Mohun was a trifle sentimental, and had in him a singular element of superstition, which led him to the study of all manner of occult subjects, although his sane mental health safeguarded him against fantastic and perilous faiths. He made daring incursions into the realm of the unreal without renouncing his residence in the partly surveyed and charted region of what we are pleased to call certitude.

The night of my visit to him was stormy. The Californian winter was on, and the incessant rain plashed in the deserted streets, or, lifted by irregular gusts of wind, was hurled against the houses with incredible fury. With no small difficulty my cabman found the right place, away out toward the ocean beach, in a sparsely populated suburb. The dwelling, a rather ugly one, apparently, stood in the centre of its grounds, which as nearly as I could make out in the gloom were destitute of either flowers or grass. Three or four trees, writhing and moaning in the torment of the tempest, appeared to be trying to escape from their dismal environment and take the chance of finding a better one out at sea. The house was a two-storey brick structure with a tower, a storey higher, at one corner. In a window of that was the only visible light. Something in the appearance of the place made me shudder, a performance that may have been assisted by a rill of rain-water down my back as I scuttled to cover in the doorway.

In answer to my note apprising him of my wish to call, Dampier had written, 'Don't ring – open the door and come up.' I did so. The staircase was dimly lighted by a single gas-jet at the top of the second flight. I managed to reach the landing without disaster and entered by an open door into the lighted square room of the tower. Dampier came forward in gown and slippers to receive me, giving me the greeting that I wished, and if I had held a thought that it might more fitly have been accorded me at the front door the first look at him dispelled any sense of his inhospitality.

He was not the same. Hardly past middle age, he had gone grey and had acquired a pronounced stoop. His figure was thin and angular, his face deeply lined, his complexion dead-white, without a touch of colour. His eyes, unnaturally large, glowed with a fire that was almost uncanny.

He seated me, proffered a cigar, and with grave and obvious sincerity assured me of the pleasure that it gave him to meet me. Some unimportant conversation followed, but all the while I was dominated by a melancholy sense of the great change in him. This he must have perceived, for he suddenly said with a bright enough smile, 'You are disappointed in me – *non sum qualis eram.*'

I hardly knew what to reply, but managed to say: 'Why, really, I don't know: your Latin is about the same.'

He brightened again. 'No,' he said, 'being a dead language, it grows in appropriateness. But please have the patience to wait: where I am going there is perhaps a better tongue. Will you care to have a message in it?'

The smile faded as he spoke, and as he concluded he was looking into my eyes with a gravity that distressed me. Yet I would not surrender myself to his mood, nor permit him to see how deeply his prescience of death affected me.

'I fancy that it will be long,' I said, 'before human speech will cease to serve our need; and then the need, with its possibilities of service, will have passed.'

He made no reply, and I too was silent, for the talk had taken a dispiriting turn, yet I knew not how to give it a more agreeable character. Suddenly, in a pause of the storm, when the dead silence was almost startling by contrast with the previous uproar, I heard a gentle tapping, which appeared to come from the wall behind my chair. The sound was such as might have been made by a human hand, not as upon a door by one asking admittance, but rather, I thought, as an agreed signal, an assurance of someone's presence in an adjoining room; most of us, I fancy, have had more experience of such communications than we should care to relate. I glanced at Dampier. If possibly there was something of amusement in the look he did not observe it. He appeared to have forgotten my presence, and was staring at the wall behind me with an expression in his eyes that I am unable to name, although my memory of it is as vivid today as was my sense of it then. The situation was embarrassing; I rose to take my leave. At this he seemed to recover himself.

'Please be seated,' he said; 'it is nothing – no one is there.'

But the tapping was repeated, and with the same gentle, slow insistence as before.

'Pardon me,' I said, 'it is late. May I call tomorrow?'

He smiled – a little mechanically, I thought. 'It is very delicate of you,' said he, 'but quite needless. Really, this is the only room in the tower, and no one is there. At least – ' He left the sentence incomplete, rose, and threw up a window, the only opening in the wall from which the sound seemed to come. 'See.'

Not clearly knowing what else to do I followed him to the window and looked out. A street-lamp some little distance away gave enough light through the murk of the rain that was again falling in torrents to make it entirely plain that 'no one was there'. In truth there was nothing but the sheer blank wall of the tower.

Dampier closed the window and signing me to my seat resumed his own.

The incident was not in itself particularly mysterious; any one of a dozen explanations was possible (though none has occurred to me), yet it impressed me strangely, the more, perhaps, from my friend's effort to reassure me, which seemed to dignify it with a certain significance and importance. He had proved that no one was there, but in that fact lay all the interest; and he proffered no explanation. His silence was irritating and made me resentful.

'My good friend,' I said, somewhat ironically, I fear, 'I am not disposed to question your right to harbour as many spooks as you find agreeable to your taste and consistent with your notions of companionship; that is no business of mine. But being just a plain man of affairs, mostly of this world, I find spooks needless to my peace and comfort. I am going to my hotel, where my fellow-guests are still in the flesh.'

It was not a very civil speech, but he manifested no feeling about it. 'Kindly remain,' he said. 'I am grateful for your presence here. What you have heard tonight I believe myself to have heard twice before. Now I *know* it was no illusion. That is much to me – more than you know. Have a fresh cigar and a good stock of patience while I tell you the story.'

The rain was now falling more steadily, with a low, monotonous susurration, interrupted at long intervals by the sudden slashing of the boughs of the trees as the wind rose and failed. The night was well advanced, but both sympathy and curiosity held me a willing listener to my friend's monologue, which I did not interrupt by a single word from beginning to end.

'Ten years ago,' he said, 'I occupied a ground-floor apartment in one of a row of houses, all alike, away at the other end of the town, on what we call Rincon Hill. This had been the best quarter of San Francisco, but had fallen into neglect and decay, partly because the primitive character of its domestic architecture no longer suited the maturing tastes of our wealthy citizens, partly because certain public improvements had made a wreck of it. The row of dwellings in one of which I lived stood a little way back from the street, each having a miniature garden, separated from its neighbours by low iron fences and bisected with mathematical precision by a box-bordered gravel walk from gate to door.

'One morning as I was leaving my lodging I observed a young girl entering the adjoining garden on the left. It was a warm day in June, and she was lightly gowned in white. From her shoulders hung a broad straw hat profusely decorated with flowers and wonderfully beribboned in the fashion of the time. My attention was not long held by the exquisite simplicity of her costume, for no one could look at her face and think of anything earthly. Do not fear; I shall not profane it by description; it was beautiful exceedingly. All that I had ever seen or dreamed of loveliness was in that matchless living picture by the hand of the Divine Artist. So deeply did it move me that, without a thought of the impropriety of the act, I unconsciously bared my head, as a devout Catholic or well-bred Protestant uncovers before an image of the Blessed Virgin. The maiden showed no displeasure; she merely turned her glorious dark eyes upon me with a look that made me catch my breath, and without other recognition of my act passed into the house. For a moment I stood motionless, hat in hand, painfully conscious of my rudeness, yet so dominated by the emotion inspired by that vision of incomparable beauty that my penitence was less poignant than it should have been. Then I went my way, leaving my heart behind. In the natural course of things I should probably have remained away until nightfall, but by the middle of the afternoon I was back in the little garden, affecting an interest in the few foolish flowers that I had never before observed. My hope was vain; she did not appear.

'To a night of unrest succeeded a day of expectation and disappointment, but on the day after, as I wandered aimlessly about the neighbourhood, I met her. Of course I did not repeat my folly of uncovering, nor venture by even so much as too long a look to manifest an interest in her; yet my heart was beating audibly. I trembled and consciously coloured as she turned her big black eyes upon me with a look of obvious recognition entirely devoid of boldness or coquetry.

'I will not weary you with particulars; many times afterward I met the maiden, yet never either addressed her or sought to fix her attention. Nor did I take any action toward making her acquaintance. Perhaps my forbearance, requiring so supreme an effort of self-denial, will not be entirely clear to you. That I was heels over head in love is true, but who can overcome his habit of thought, or reconstruct his character?

'I was what some foolish persons are pleased to call, and others, more foolish, are pleased to be called – an aristocrat; and despite her beauty, her charms and grace, the girl was not of my class. I had learned her name – which it is needless to speak – and something of her family. She was an orphan, a dependent niece of the impossible elderly fat woman in whose lodging-house she lived. My income was small and I lacked the talent for marrying; it is perhaps a gift. An alliance with that family would condemn me to its manner of life, part me from my books and studies, and in a social sense reduce me to the ranks. It is easy to deprecate such considerations as these and I have not retained myself for the defence. Let judgement be entered against me, but in strict justice all my ancestors for generations should be made co-defendants and I be permitted to plead in mitigation of punishment the imperious mandate of heredity. To a *mésalliance* of that kind every globule of my ancestral blood spoke in opposition. In brief, my tastes, habits, instinct, with whatever of reason my love had left me – all fought against it. Moreover, I was an irreclaimable sentimentalist, and found a subtle charm in an impersonal and spiritual relation which acquaintance might vulgarise and marriage would certainly dispel. No woman, I argued, is what this lovely creature seems. Love is a delicious dream; why should I bring about my own awakening?

'The course dictated by all this sense and sentiment was obvious. Honour, pride, prudence, preservation of my ideals – all commanded me to go away, but for that I was too weak. The utmost that I could do by a mighty effort of will was to cease meeting the girl, and that I did. I even avoided the chance encounters of the garden, leaving my lodging only when I knew that she had gone to her music lessons, and returning after nightfall. Yet all the while I was as one in a trance, indulging the most fascinating fancies and ordering my entire intellectual life in accordance with my dream. Ah, my friend, as one whose actions have a traceable relation to reason, you cannot know the fool's paradise in which I lived.

'One evening the devil put it into my head to be an unspeakable idiot. By apparently careless and purposeless questioning I learned from my gossipy landlady that the young woman's bedroom adjoined my own, a party-wall between. Yielding to a sudden and coarse impulse I gently rapped on the wall. There was no response, naturally, but I was in no mood to accept a rebuke. A madness was upon me and I repeated the folly, the offence, but again ineffectually, and I had the decency to desist.

'An hour later, while absorbed in some of my infernal studies, I heard, or thought I heard, my signal answered. Flinging down my books I sprang to the wall and as steadily as my beating heart would permit gave three slow taps upon it. This time the response was distinct, unmistakable: one, two, three – an exact repetition of my signal. That was all I could elicit, but it was enough – too much.

'The next evening, and for many evenings afterward, that folly went on, I always having "the last word". During the whole period I was deliriously happy, but with the perversity of my nature I persevered in my resolution not to see her. Then, as I should have expected, I got no further answers. "She is disgusted," I said to myself, "with what she thinks my timidity in making no more definite advances"; and I resolved to seek her and make her acquaintance and – what? I did not know, nor do I now know, what might have come of it. I know only that I passed days and days trying to meet her, and all in vain; she was invisible as well as inaudible. I haunted the streets where we had met, but she did not come. From my window I watched the garden in front of her house, but she passed neither in nor out. I fell into the deepest dejection, believing that she had gone away, yet took no steps to resolve my doubt by inquiry of my landlady, to whom, indeed, I had taken an

unconquerable aversion from her having once spoken of the girl with
less of reverence than I thought befitting.

'There came a fateful night. Worn out with emotion, irresolution and
despondency, I had retired early and fallen into such sleep as was still
possible to me. In the middle of the night something – some malign
power bent upon the wrecking of my peace for ever – caused me to
open my eyes and sit up, wide awake and listening intently for I knew
not what. Then I thought I heard a faint tapping on the wall – the mere
ghost of the familiar signal. In a few moments it was repeated: one, two,
three – no louder than before, but addressing a sense alert and strained
to receive it. I was about to reply when the Adversary of Peace again
intervened in my affairs with a rascally suggestion of retaliation. She had
long and cruelly ignored me; now I would ignore her. Incredible
fatuity – may God forgive it! All the rest of the night I lay awake,
fortifying my obstinacy with shameless justifications and – listening.

'Late the next morning, as I was leaving the house, I met my
landlady, entering.

' "Good-morning, Mr Dampier," she said. "Have you heard the
news?"

'I replied in words that I had heard no news; in manner, that I did not
care to hear any. The manner escaped her observation.

' "About the sick young lady next door," she babbled on. "What! you
did not know? Why, she has been ill for weeks. And now – "

'I almost sprang upon her. "And now," I cried, "now what?"

' "She is dead."

'That is not the whole story. In the middle of the night, as I learned
later, the patient, awakening from a long stupor after a week of
delirium, had asked – it was her last utterance – that her bed be moved
to the opposite side of the room. Those in attendance had thought the
request a vagary of her delirium, but had complied. And there the poor
passing soul had exerted its failing will to restore a broken connection –
a golden thread of sentiment between its innocence and a monstrous
baseness owning a blind, brutal allegiance to the Law of Self.

'What reparation could I make? Are there masses that can be said for
the repose of souls that are abroad such nights as this – spirits "blown
about by the viewless winds" – coming in the storm and darkness with
signs and portents, hints of memory and presages of doom?

'This is the third visitation. On the first occasion I was too sceptical
to do more than verify by natural methods the character of the
incident; on the second, responded to the signal after it had been
several times repeated, but without result. Tonight's recurrence

completes the "fatal triad" expounded by Parapelius Necromantius. There is no more to tell.'

When Dampier had finished his story I could think of nothing relevant that I cared to say, and to question him would have been a hideous impertinence. I rose and bade him good-night in a way to convey to him a sense of my sympathy, which he silently acknowledged by a pressure of the hand. That night, alone with his sorrow and remorse, he passed into the Unknown.

A Psychological Shipwreck

In the summer of 1874 I was in Liverpool, whither I had gone on business for the mercantile house of Bronson & Jarrett, New York. I am William Jarrett; my partner was Zenas Bronson. The firm failed last year, and unable to endure the fall from affluence to poverty he died.

Having finished my business, and feeling the lassitude and exhaustion incident to its dispatch, I felt that a protracted sea voyage would be both agreeable and beneficial, so instead of embarking for my return on one of the many fine passenger steamers I booked for New York on the sailing vessel *Morrow*, upon which I had shipped a large and valuable invoice of the goods I had bought. The *Morrow* was an English ship with, of course, but little accommodation for passengers, of whom there were only myself, a young woman and her servant, who was a middle-aged negress. I thought it singular that a travelling English girl should be so attended, but she afterward explained to me that the woman had been left with her family by a man and his wife from South Carolina, both of whom had died on the same day at the house of the young lady's father in Devonshire – a circumstance in itself sufficiently uncommon to remain rather distinctly in my memory, even had it not afterward transpired in conversation with the young lady that the name of the man was William Jarrett, the same as my own. I knew that a branch of my family had settled in South Carolina, but of them and their history I was ignorant.

The *Morrow* sailed from the mouth of the Mersey on the 15th of June, and for several weeks we had fair breezes and unclouded skies. The skipper, an admirable seaman but nothing more, favoured us with very little of his society, except at his table; and the young woman, Miss Janette Harford, and I became very well acquainted. We were, in truth, nearly always together, and being of an introspective turn of mind I often endeavoured to analyse and define the novel feeling with which she inspired me – a secret, subtle, but powerful attraction which constantly impelled me to seek her; but the attempt was hopeless. I could only be sure that at least it was not love. Having assured myself of this and being certain that she was quite as wholehearted, I ventured one evening (I remember it was on the 3rd of July) as we sat on deck to ask her, laughingly, if she could assist me to resolve my psychological doubt.

For a moment she was silent, with averted face, and I began to fear I had been extremely rude and indelicate; then she fixed her eyes gravely on my own. In an instant my mind was dominated by as strange a fancy as ever entered human consciousness. It seemed as if she were looking at me, not *with*, but *through*, those eyes from an immeasurable distance behind them – and that a number of other persons, men, women and children, upon whose faces I caught strangely familiar evanescent expressions, clustered about her, struggling with gentle eagerness to look at me through the same orbs. Ship, ocean, sky – all had vanished. I was conscious of nothing but the figures in this extraordinary and fantastic scene. Then all at once darkness fell upon me, and anon from out of it, as to one who grows accustomed by degrees to a dimmer light, my former surroundings of deck and mast and cordage slowly resolved themselves. Miss Harford had closed her eyes and was leaning back in her chair, apparently asleep, the book she had been reading open in her lap. Impelled by surely I cannot say what motive, I glanced at the top of the page; it was a copy of that rare and curious work, Denneker's *Meditations*, and the lady's index finger rested on this passage:

> To sundry it is given to be drawn away, and to be apart from the body for a season; for, as concerning rills which would flow across each other the weaker is borne along by the stronger, so there be certain of kin whose paths intersecting, their souls do bear company, the while their bodies go fore-appointed ways, unknowing.

Miss Harford arose, shuddering; the sun had sunk below the horizon, but it was not cold. There was not a breath of wind; there were no clouds in the sky, yet not a star was visible. A hurried tramping sounded on the deck; the captain, summoned from below, joined the first officer, who stood looking at the barometer. 'Good God!' I heard him exclaim.

An hour later the form of Janette Harford, invisible in the darkness and spray, was torn from my grasp by the cruel vortex of the sinking ship, and I fainted in the cordage of the floating mast to which I had lashed myself.

It was by lamplight that I awoke. I lay in a berth amid the familiar surroundings of the state-room of a steamer. On a couch opposite sat a man, half undressed for bed, reading a book. I recognised the face of my friend Gordon Doyle, whom I had met in Liverpool on the day of my embarkation, when he was himself about to sail on the steamer *City of Prague*, on which he had urged me to accompany him.

After some moments I now spoke his name. He simply said, 'Well,' and turned a leaf in his book without removing his eyes from the page.

'Doyle,' I repeated, 'did they save *her*?'

He now deigned to look at me and smiled as if amused. He evidently thought me but half awake.

'Her? Whom do you mean?'

'Janette Harford.'

His amusement turned to amazement; he stared at me fixedly, saying nothing.

'You will tell me after a while,' I continued; 'I suppose you will tell me after a while.'

A moment later I asked: 'What ship is this?'

Doyle stared again. 'The steamer *City of Prague*, bound from Liverpool to New York, three weeks out with a broken shaft. Principal passenger, Mr Gordon Doyle; ditto lunatic, Mr William Jarrett. These two distinguished travellers embarked together, but they are about to part, it being the resolute intention of the former to pitch the latter overboard.'

I sat bolt upright. 'Do you mean to say that I have been for three weeks a passenger on this steamer?'

'Yes, pretty nearly; this is the 3rd of July.'

'Have I been ill?'

'Right as a trivet all the time, and punctual at your meals.'

'My God! Doyle, there is some mystery here; do have the goodness to be serious. Was I not rescued from the wreck of the ship *Morrow*?'

Doyle changed colour, and approaching me, laid his fingers on my wrist. A moment later, 'What do you know of Janette Harford?' he asked very calmly.

'First tell me what you know of her?'

Mr Doyle gazed at me for some moments as if thinking what to do, then seating himself again on the couch, said: 'Why should I not? I am engaged to marry Janette Harford, whom I met a year ago in London. Her family, one of the wealthiest in Devonshire, cut up rough about it, and we eloped – are eloping rather, for on the day that you and I walked to the landing stage to go aboard this steamer she and her faithful servant, a negress, passed us, driving to the ship *Morrow*. She would not consent to go in the same vessel with me, and it had been deemed best that she take a sailing vessel in order to avoid observation and lessen the risk of detection. I am now alarmed lest this cursed breaking of our machinery may detain us so long that the *Morrow* will get to New York before us, and the poor girl will not know where to go.'

I lay still in my berth – so still I hardly breathed. But the subject was evidently not displeasing to Doyle, and after a short pause he resumed: 'By the way, she is only an adopted daughter of the Harfords. Her mother was killed at their place by being thrown from a horse while hunting, and her father, mad with grief, made away with himself the same day. No one ever claimed the child, and after a reasonable time they adopted her. She has grown up in the belief that she is their daughter.'

'Doyle, what book are you reading?'

'Oh, it's called Denneker's *Meditations*. It's a rum lot, Janette gave it to me; she happened to have two copies. Want to see it?'

He tossed me the volume, which opened as it fell. On one of the exposed pages was a marked passage:

> To sundry it is given to be drawn away, and to be apart from the body for a season; for, as concerning rills which would flow across each other the weaker is borne along by the stronger, so there be certain of kin whose paths intersecting, their souls do bear company, the while their bodies go fore-appointed ways, unknowing.

'She had – she has – a singular taste in reading,' I managed to say, mastering my agitation.

'Yes. And now perhaps you will have the kindness to explain how you knew her name and that of the ship she sailed in.'

'You talked of her in your sleep,' I said.

A week later we were towed into the port of New York. But the *Morrow* was never heard from.

The Middle Toe of the Right Foot

It is well known that the old Manton house is haunted. In all the rural district near about, and even in the town of Marshall, a mile away, not one person of unbiased mind entertains a doubt of it; incredulity is confined to those opinionated persons who will be called 'cranks' as soon as the useful word shall have penetrated the intellectual demesne of the Marshall *Advance*. The evidence that the house is haunted is of two kinds: the testimony of disinterested witnesses who have had ocular proof, and that of the house itself. The former may be disregarded and ruled out on any of the various grounds of objection which may be urged against it by the ingenious; but facts within the observation of all are material and controlling.

In the first place, the Manton house has been unoccupied by mortals for more than ten years, and with its outbuildings is slowly falling into decay – a circumstance which in itself the judicious will hardly venture to ignore. It stands a little way off the loneliest reach of the Marshall and Harriston road, in an opening which was once a farm and is still disfigured with strips of rotting fence and half covered with brambles overrunning a stony and sterile soil long unacquainted with the plough. The house itself is in tolerably good condition, though badly weather-stained and in dire need of attention from the glazier, the smaller male population of the region having attested in the manner of its kind its disapproval of dwelling without dwellers. It is two storeys in height, nearly square, its front pierced by a single doorway flanked on each side by a window boarded up to the very top. Corresponding windows above, not protected, serve to admit light and rain to the rooms of the upper floor. Grass and weeds grow pretty rankly all about, and a few shade trees, somewhat the worse for wind, and leaning all in one direction, seem to be making a concerted effort to run away. In short, as the Marshall town humorist explained in the columns of the *Advance*, 'the proposition that the Manton house is badly haunted is the only logical conclusion from the premises'. The fact that in this dwelling Mr Manton thought it expedient one night some ten years ago to rise and cut the throats of his wife and two small children, removing at once to another part of the country, has no doubt done its share in directing public attention to the fitness of the place for supernatural phenomena.

To this house, one summer evening, came four men in a wagon. Three of them promptly alighted, and the one who had been driving hitched the team to the only remaining post of what had been a fence. The fourth remained seated in the wagon. 'Come,' said one of his companions, approaching him, while the others moved away in the direction of the dwelling – 'this is the place.'

The man addressed did not move. 'By God!' he said harshly, 'this is a trick, and it looks to me as if you were in it.'

'Perhaps I am,' the other said, looking him straight in the face and speaking in a tone which had something of contempt in it. 'You will remember, however, that the choice of place was with your own assent left to the other side. Of course if you are afraid of spooks – '

'I am afraid of nothing,' the man interrupted with another oath, and sprang to the ground. The two then joined the others at the door, which one of them had already opened with some difficulty, caused by rust of lock and hinge. All entered. Inside it was dark, but the man who had unlocked the door produced a candle and matches and made a light. He then unlocked a door on their right as they stood in the passage. This gave them entrance to a large, square room that the candle but dimly lighted. The floor had a thick carpeting of dust, which partly muffled their footfalls. Cobwebs were in the angles of the walls and depended from the ceiling like strips of rotting lace, making undulatory movements in the disturbed air. The room had two windows in adjoining sides, but from neither could anything be seen except the rough inner surfaces of boards a few inches from the glass. There was no fireplace, no furniture; there was nothing: besides the cobwebs and the dust, the four men were the only objects there which were not a part of the structure.

Strange enough they looked in the yellow light of the candle. The one who had so reluctantly alighted was especially spectacular – he might have been called sensational. He was of middle age, heavily built, deep chested and broad shouldered. Looking at his figure, one would have said that he had a giant's strength; at his features, that he would use it like a giant. He was clean shaven, his hair rather closely cropped and grey. His low forehead was seamed with wrinkles above the eyes, and over the nose these became vertical. The heavy black brows followed the same law, saved from meeting only by an upward turn at what would otherwise have been the point of contact. Deeply sunken beneath these, glowed in the obscure light a pair of eyes of uncertain colour, but obviously enough too small. There was something forbidding in their expression, which was not bettered by the cruel mouth and wide jaw. The nose was well enough, as noses go; one does not expect much of noses. All that was sinister in the man's face seemed accentuated by an unnatural pallor – he appeared altogether bloodless.

The appearance of the other men was sufficiently commonplace: they were such persons as one meets and forgets that he met. All were younger than the man described, between whom and the eldest of the others, who stood apart, there was apparently no kindly feeling. They avoided looking at each other.

'Gentlemen,' said the man holding the candle and keys, 'I believe everything is right. Are you ready, Mr Rosser?'

The man standing apart from the group bowed and smiled.

'And you, Mr Grossmith?'

The heavy man bowed and scowled.

'You will be pleased to remove your outer clothing.'

Their hats, coats, waistcoats and neckwear were soon removed and thrown outside the door, in the passage. The man with the candle now nodded, and the fourth man – he who had urged Grossmith to leave the wagon – produced from the pocket of his overcoat two long, murderous-looking bowie-knives, which he drew now from their leather scabbards.

'They are exactly alike,' he said, presenting one to each of the two principals – for by this time the dullest observer would have understood the nature of this meeting. It was to be a duel to the death.

Each combatant took a knife, examined it critically near the candle and tested the strength of blade and handle across his lifted knee. Their persons were then searched in turn, each by the second of the other.

'If it is agreeable to you, Mr Grossmith,' said the man holding the light, 'you will place yourself in that corner.'

He indicated the angle of the room farthest from the door, whither Grossmith retired, his second parting from him with a grasp of the hand which had nothing of cordiality in it. In the angle nearest the door Mr Rosser stationed himself, and after a whispered consultation his second left him, joining the other near the door. At that moment the candle was suddenly extinguished, leaving all in profound darkness. This may have been done by a draught from the opened door; whatever the cause, the effect was startling.

'Gentlemen,' said a voice which sounded strangely unfamiliar in the altered condition affecting the relations of the senses – 'gentlemen, you will not move until you hear the closing of the outer door.'

A sound of trampling ensued, then the closing of the inner door; and finally the outer one closed with a concussion which shook the entire building.

A few minutes afterward a belated farmer's boy met a light wagon which was being driven furiously toward the town of Marshall. He declared that behind the two figures on the front seat stood a third, with its hands upon the bowed shoulders of the others, who appeared to struggle vainly to free themselves from its grasp. This figure, unlike the others, was clad in white, and had undoubtedly boarded the wagon as it passed the haunted house. As the lad could boast a considerable former experience with the supernatural thereabouts his word had the weight justly due to the testimony of an expert. The story (in connection with the next day's events) eventually appeared in the *Advance*, with some slight literary embellishments and a concluding intimation that the gentlemen referred to would be allowed the use of the paper's columns for their version of the night's adventure. But the privilege remained without a claimant.

❧ TWO ❧

The events that led up to this 'duel in the dark' were simple enough. One evening three young men of the town of Marshall were sitting in a quiet corner of the porch of the village hotel, smoking and discussing such matters as three educated young men of a Southern village would naturally find interesting. Their names were King, Sancher and Rosser. At a little distance, within easy hearing, but taking no part in the conversation, sat a fourth. He was a stranger to the others. They merely knew that on his arrival by the stagecoach that afternoon he had written in the hotel register the name Robert Grossmith. He had not been observed to speak to anyone except the hotel clerk. He seemed, indeed, singularly fond of his own company – or, as the *personnel* of the *Advance* expressed it, 'grossly addicted to evil associations'. But then it should be said in justice to the stranger that the *personnel* was himself of a too convivial disposition fairly to judge one differently gifted, and had, moreover, experienced a slight rebuff in an effort at an 'interview'.

'I hate any kind of deformity in a woman,' said King, 'whether natural or – acquired. I have a theory that any physical defect has its correlative mental and moral defect.'

'I infer, then,' said Rosser gravely, 'that a lady lacking the moral advantage of a nose would find the struggle to become Mrs King an arduous enterprise.'

'Of course you may put it that way,' was the reply; 'but, seriously, I once threw over a most charming girl on learning quite accidentally that she had suffered amputation of a toe. My conduct was brutal if you like, but if I had married that girl I should have been miserable for life and should have made her so.'

'Whereas,' said Sancher, with a light laugh, 'by marrying a gentleman of more liberal views she escaped with a parted throat.'

'Ah, you know to whom I refer. Yes, she married Manton, but I don't know about his liberality; I'm not sure but he cut her throat because he discovered that she lacked that excellent thing in woman, the middle toe of the right foot.'

'Look at that chap!' said Rosser in a low voice, his eyes fixed upon the stranger.

'That chap' was obviously listening intently to the conversation.

'Damn his impudence!' muttered King – 'what ought we to do?'

'That's an easy one,' Rosser replied, rising. 'Sir,' he continued, addressing the stranger, 'I think it would be better if you would remove your chair to the other end of the veranda. The presence of gentlemen is evidently an unfamiliar situation to you.'

The man sprang to his feet and strode forward with clenched hands, his face white with rage. All were now standing. Sancher stepped between the belligerents.

'You are hasty and unjust,' he said to Rosser; 'this gentleman has done nothing to deserve such language.'

But Rosser would not withdraw a word. By the custom of the country and the time there could be but one outcome to the quarrel.

'I demand the satisfaction due to a gentleman,' said the stranger, who had become more calm. 'I have not an acquaintance in this region. Perhaps you, sir,' bowing to Sancher, 'will be kind enough to represent me in this matter.'

Sancher accepted the trust – somewhat reluctantly it must be confessed, for the man's appearance and manner were not at all to his liking. King, who during the colloquy had hardly removed his eyes from the stranger's face and had not spoken a word, consented with a nod to act for Rosser, and the upshot of it was that, the principals having retired, a meeting was arranged for the next evening. The nature of the arrangements has been already disclosed. The duel with knives in a dark room was once a commoner feature of south-western life than it is likely to be again. How thin a veneering of 'chivalry' covered the essential brutality of the code under which such encounters were possible we shall see.

◆§ THREE §◆

In the blaze of a midsummer noonday the old Manton house was hardly true to its traditions. It was of the earth, earthy. The sunshine caressed it warmly and affectionately, with evident disregard of its bad reputation. The grass greening all the expanse in its front seemed to grow, not rankly, but with a natural and joyous exuberance, and the weeds blossomed quite like plants. Full of charming lights and shadows and populous with pleasant-voiced birds, the neglected shade trees no longer struggled to run away, but bent reverently beneath their burden of sun and song. Even in the glassless upper windows was an expression of peace and contentment, due to the light within. Over the stony fields the visible heat danced with a lively tremor incompatible with the gravity which is an attribute of the supernatural.

Such was the aspect under which the place presented itself to Sheriff Adams and two other men who had come out from Marshall to look at it. One of these men was Mr King, the sheriff's deputy; the other, whose name was Brewer, was a brother of the late Mrs Manton. Under a beneficent law of the State relating to property which had been for a certain period abandoned by an owner whose residence cannot be ascertained, the sheriff was legal custodian of the Manton farm and appurtenances thereunto belonging. His present visit was in mere perfunctory compliance with some order of a court in which Mr Brewer had an action to get possession of the property as heir to his deceased sister. By a mere coincidence, the visit was made on the day after the night that Deputy King had unlocked the house for another and very different purpose. His presence now was not of his own choosing: he had been ordered to accompany his superior, and at the

moment could think of nothing more prudent than simulated alacrity
in obedience to the command.

Carelessly opening the front door, which to his surprise was not
locked, the sheriff was amazed to see, lying on the floor of the passage
into which it opened, a confused heap of men's apparel. Examination
showed it to consist of two hats, and the same number of coats,
waistcoats and scarves, all in a remarkably good state of preservation,
albeit somewhat defiled by the dust in which they lay. Mr Brewer was
equally astonished, but Mr King's emotion is not on record. With a new
and lively interest in his own actions the sheriff now unlatched and
pushed open the door on the right, and the three entered. The room
was apparently vacant – no; as their eyes became accustomed to the
dimmer light something was visible in the farthest angle of the wall. It
was a human figure – that of a man crouching close in the corner.
Something in the attitude made the intruders halt when they had barely
passed the threshold. The figure more and more clearly defined itself.
The man was upon one knee, his back in the angle of the wall, his
shoulders elevated to the level of his ears, his hands before his face,
palms outward, the fingers spread and crooked like claws; the white face
turned upward on the retracted neck had an expression of unutterable
fright, the mouth half open, the eyes incredibly expanded. He was stone
dead. Yet, with the exception of a bowie-knife, which had evidently
fallen from his own hand, not another object was in the room.

In thick dust that covered the floor were some confused footprints
near the door and along the wall through which it opened. Along one of
the adjoining walls, too, past the boarded-up windows, was the trail
made by the man himself in reaching his corner. Instinctively in
approaching the body the three men followed that trail. The sheriff
grasped one of the out-thrown arms; it was as rigid as iron, and the
application of a gentle force rocked the entire body without altering the
relation of its parts. Brewer, pale with excitement, gazed intently into
the distorted face. 'God of mercy!' he suddenly cried, 'it is Manton!'

'You are right,' said King, with an evident attempt at calmness: 'I
knew Manton. He then wore a full beard and his hair long, but this
is he.'

He might have added: 'I recognised him when he challenged Rosser.
I told Rosser and Sancher who he was before we played him this
horrible trick. When Rosser left this dark room at our heels, forgetting
his outer clothing in the excitement, and driving away with us in his
shirt sleeves – all through the discreditable proceedings we knew whom
we were dealing with, murderer and coward that he was!'

But nothing of this did Mr King say. With his better light he was trying to penetrate the mystery of the man's death. That he had not once moved from the corner where he had been stationed; that his posture was that of neither attack nor defence; that he had dropped his weapon; that he had obviously perished of sheer horror of something that he *saw* – these were circumstances which Mr King's disturbed intelligence could not rightly comprehend.

Groping in intellectual darkness for a clue to his maze of doubt, his gaze, directed mechanically downward in the way of one who ponders momentous matters, fell upon something which, there, in the light of day and in the presence of living companions, affected him with terror. In the dust of years that lay thick upon the floor – leading from the door by which they had entered, straight across the room to within a yard of Manton's crouching corpse – were three parallel lines of footprints – light but definite impressions of bare feet, the outer ones those of small children, the inner a woman's. From the point at which they ended they did not return; they pointed all one way. Brewer, who had observed them at the same moment, was leaning forward in an attitude of rapt attention, horribly pale.

'Look at that!' he cried, pointing with both hands at the nearest print of the woman's right foot, where she had apparently stopped and stood. 'The middle toe is missing – it was Gertrude!'

Gertrude was the late Mrs Manton, sister of Mr Brewer.

John Mortonson's Funeral

Rough notes of this tale were found among the papers of
the late Leigh Bierce. It is printed here with such revision
only as the author might himself have made in transcription.

John Mortonson was dead: his lines in the tragedy *Man* had all been
spoken and he had left the stage.

The body rested in a fine mahogany coffin fitted with a plate of glass.
All arrangements for the funeral had been so well attended to that had
the deceased known he would doubtless have approved. The face, as it
showed under the glass, was not disagreeable to look upon: it bore a
faint smile, and as the death had been painless, had not been distorted
beyond the repairing power of the undertaker. At two o'clock of the
afternoon the friends were to assemble to pay their last tribute of
respect to one who had no further need of friends and respect. The
surviving members of the family came severally every few minutes to
the casket and wept above the placid features beneath the glass. This
did them no good; it did no good to John Mortonson; but in the
presence of death reason and philosophy are silent.

As the hour of two approached the friends began to arrive and after
offering such consolation to the stricken relatives as the proprieties of
the occasion required, solemnly seated themselves about the room with
an augmented consciousness of their importance in the scheme funereal. Then the minister came, and in that overshadowing presence the
lesser lights went into eclipse. His entrance was followed by that of the
widow, whose lamentations filled the room. She approached the casket
and after leaning her face against the cold glass for a moment was
gently led to a seat near her daughter. Mournfully and low the man of
God began his eulogy of the dead, and his doleful voice, mingled with
the sobbing which it was its purpose to stimulate and sustain, rose and
fell, seemed to come and go, like the sound of a sullen sea. The gloomy

day grew darker as he spoke; a curtain of cloud underspread the sky and a few drops of rain fell audibly. It seemed as if all nature were weeping for John Mortonson.

When the minister had finished his eulogy with prayer a hymn was sung and the pall-bearers took their places beside the bier. As the last notes of the hymn died away the widow ran to the coffin, cast herself upon it and sobbed hysterically. Gradually, however, she yielded to dissuasion, becoming more composed; and as the minister was in the act of leading her away her eyes sought the face of the dead beneath the glass. She threw up her arms and with a shriek fell backward insensible.

The mourners sprang forward to the coffin, the friends followed, and as the clock on the mantel solemnly struck three all were staring down upon the face of John Mortonson, deceased.

They turned away, sick and faint. One man, trying in his terror to escape the awful sight, stumbled against the coffin so heavily as to knock away one of its frail supports. The coffin fell to the floor, the glass was shattered to bits by the concussion.

From the opening crawled John Mortonson's cat, which lazily leapt to the floor, sat up, tranquilly wiped its crimson muzzle with a forepaw, then walked with dignity from the room.

The Realm of the Unreal

ONE

For a part of the distance between Auburn and Newcastle the road –
first on one side of a creek and then on the other – occupies the whole
bottom of the ravine, being partly cut out of the steep hillside, and
partly built up with boulders removed from the creek-bed by the
miners. The hills are wooded, the course of the ravine is sinuous. In a
dark night careful driving is required in order not to go off into the
water. The night that I have in memory was dark, the creek a torrent,
swollen by a recent storm. I had driven up from Newcastle and was
within about a mile of Auburn in the darkest and narrowest part of the
ravine, looking intently ahead of my horse for the roadway. Suddenly I
saw a man almost under the animal's nose, and reined in with a jerk
that came near setting the creature upon its haunches.

'I beg your pardon,' I said; 'I did not see you, sir.'

'You could hardly be expected to see me,' the man replied civilly,
approaching the side of the vehicle; 'and the noise of the creek
prevented my hearing you.'

I at once recognised the voice, although five years had passed since I
had heard it. I was not particularly well pleased to hear it now.

'You are Dr Dorrimore, I think,' said I.

'Yes; and you are my good friend Mr Manrich. I am more than glad
to see you – the excess,' he added, with a light laugh, 'being due to the
fact that I am going your way, and naturally expect an invitation to ride
with you.'

'Which I extend with all my heart.'

That was not altogether true.

Dr Dorrimore thanked me as he seated himself beside me, and I
drove cautiously forward, as before. Doubtless it is fancy, but it seems
to me now that the remaining distance was made in a chill fog; that I
was uncomfortably cold; that the way was longer than ever before, and

the town, when we reached it, cheerless, forbidding, and desolate. It must have been early in the evening, yet I do not recollect a light in any of the houses nor a living thing in the streets. Dorrimore explained at some length how he happened to be there, and where he had been during the years that had elapsed since I had seen him. I recall the fact of the narrative, but none of the facts narrated. He had been in foreign countries and had returned – this is all that my memory retains, and this I already knew. As to myself I cannot remember that I spoke a word, though doubtless I did.

Of one thing I am distinctly conscious: the man's presence at my side was strangely distasteful and disquieting – so much so that when I at last pulled up under the lights of the Putnam House I experienced a sense of having escaped some spiritual peril of a nature peculiarly forbidding. This sense of relief was somewhat modified by the discovery that Dr Dorrimore was living at the same hotel.

❧ TWO ☙

In partial explanation of my feelings regarding Dr Dorrimore I will relate briefly the circumstances under which I had met him some years before. One evening a half-dozen men of whom I was one were sitting in the library of the Bohemian Club in San Francisco. The conversation had turned to the subject of sleight-of-hand and the feats of the *prestidigitateurs*, one of whom was then exhibiting at a local theatre.

'These fellows are pretenders in a double sense,' said one of the party; 'they can do nothing which it is worth one's while to be made a dupe by. The humblest wayside juggler in India could mystify them to the verge of lunacy.'

'For example, how?' asked another, lighting a cigar.

'For example, by all their common and familiar performances – throwing large objects into the air which never come down; causing plants to sprout, grow visibly and blossom, in bare ground chosen by spectators; putting a man into a wicker basket, piercing him through and through with a sword while he shrieks and bleeds, and then – the basket being opened nothing is there; tossing the free end of a silken ladder into the air, mounting it and disappearing.'

'Nonsense!' I said, rather uncivilly, I fear. 'You surely do not believe such things?'

'Certainly not: I have seen them too often.'

'But I do,' said a journalist of considerable local fame as a picturesque reporter. 'I have so frequently related them that nothing but observation could shake my conviction. Why, gentlemen, I have my own word for it.'

Nobody laughed – all were looking at something behind me. Turning in my seat I saw a man in evening dress who had just entered the room. He was exceedingly dark, almost swarthy, with a thin face, black-bearded to the lips, an abundance of coarse black hair in some disorder, a high nose and eyes that glittered with as soulless an expression as those of a cobra. One of the group rose and introduced him as Dr Dorrimore, of Calcutta. As each of us was presented in turn he acknowledged the fact with a profound bow in the Oriental manner, but with nothing of Oriental gravity. His smile impressed me as cynical and a trifle contemptuous. His whole demeanour I can describe only as disagreeably engaging.

His presence led the conversation into other channels. He said little – I do not recall anything of what he did say. I thought his voice singularly rich and melodious, but it affected me in the same way as his eyes and smile. In a few minutes I rose to go. He also rose and put on his overcoat.

'Mr Manrich,' he said, 'I am going your way.'

'The devil you are!' I thought. 'How do you know which way I am going?' Then I said, 'I shall be pleased to have your company.'

We left the building together. No cabs were in sight, the street cars had gone to bed, there was a full moon and the cool night air was delightful; we walked up the California Street Hill. I took that direction thinking he would naturally wish to take another, toward one of the hotels.

'You do not believe what is told of the Hindu jugglers,' he said abruptly.

'How do you know that?' I asked.

Without replying he laid his hand lightly upon my arm and with the other pointed to the stone sidewalk directly in front. There, almost at our feet, lay the dead body of a man, the face upturned and white in the moonlight! A sword whose hilt sparkled with gems stood fixed and upright in the breast; a pool of blood had collected on the stones of the sidewalk.

I was startled and terrified – not only by what I saw, but by the circumstances under which I saw it. Repeatedly during our ascent of the hill my eyes, I thought, had traversed the whole reach of that sidewalk, from street to street. How could they have been insensible to this dreadful object now so conspicuous in the white moonlight.

As my dazed faculties cleared I observed that the body was in evening dress; the overcoat thrown wide open revealed the dress-coat, the white tie, the broad expanse of shirt front pierced by the sword. And – horrible revelation! – the face, except for its pallor, was that of my companion! It was to the minutest detail of dress and feature Dr Dorrimore himself. Bewildered and horrified, I turned to look for the living man. He was nowhere visible, and with an added terror I retired from the place, down the hill in the direction whence I had come. I had taken but a few strides when a strong grasp upon my shoulder arrested me. I came near crying out with terror: the dead man, the sword still fixed in his breast, stood beside me! Pulling out the sword with his disengaged hand, he flung it from him, the moonlight glinting upon the jewels of its hilt and the unsullied steel of its blade. It fell with a clang upon the sidewalk ahead and – vanished! The man, swarthy as before, relaxed his grasp upon my shoulder and looked at me with the same cynical regard that I had observed on first meeting him. The dead have not that look – it partly restored me, and turning my head backward, I saw the smooth white expanse of sidewalk, unbroken from street to street.

'What is all this nonsense, you devil?' I demanded, fiercely enough, though weak and trembling in every limb.

'It is what some are pleased to call jugglery,' he answered, with a light, hard laugh.

He turned down Dupont Street and I saw him no more until we met in the Auburn ravine.

❦ THREE ❦

On the day after my second meeting with Dr Dorrimore I did not see him: the clerk in the Putnam House explained that a slight illness confined him to his rooms. That afternoon at the railway station I was surprised and made happy by the unexpected arrival of Miss Margaret Corray and her mother, from Oakland.

This is not a love story. I am no storyteller, and love as it is cannot be portrayed in a literature dominated and enthralled by the debasing tyranny which 'sentences letters' in the name of the Young Girl. Under

the Young Girl's blighting reign – or rather under the rule of those
false Ministers of the Censure who have appointed themselves to the
custody of her welfare – Love

> veils her sacred fires,
> And, unaware, Morality expires,

famished upon the sifted meal and distilled water of a prudish
purveyance.

Let it suffice that Miss Corray and I were engaged in marriage. She
and her mother went to the hotel at which I lived, and for two weeks I
saw her daily. That I was happy needs hardly be said; the only bar to
my perfect enjoyment of those golden days was the presence of Dr
Dorrimore, whom I had felt compelled to introduce to the ladies.

By them he was evidently held in favour. What could I say? I knew
absolutely nothing to his discredit. His manners were those of a
cultivated and considerate gentleman; and to women a man's manner is
the man. On one or two occasions when I saw Miss Corray walking
with him I was furious, and once had the indiscretion to protest. Asked
for reasons, I had none to give, and fancied I saw in her expression a
shade of contempt for the vagaries of a jealous mind. In time I grew
morose and consciously disagreeable, and resolved in my madness to
return to San Francisco the next day. Of this, however, I said nothing.

◆ FOUR ◆

There was at Auburn an old, abandoned cemetery. It was nearly in the
heart of the town, yet by night it was as gruesome a place as the most
dismal of human moods could crave. The railings about the plots were
prostrate, decayed, or altogether gone. Many of the graves were
sunken, from others grew sturdy pines, whose roots had committed
unspeakable sin. The headstones were fallen and broken across;
brambles overran the ground; the fence was mostly gone, and cows and
pigs wandered there at will; the place was a dishonour to the living, a
calumny on the dead, a blasphemy against God.

The evening of the day on which I had taken my madman's
resolution to depart in anger from all that was dear to me found me in
that congenial spot. The light of the half moon fell ghostly through

the foliage of trees in spots and patches, revealing much that was unsightly, and the black shadows seemed conspiracies withholding to the proper time revelations of darker import. Passing along what had been a gravel path, I saw emerging from shadow the figure of Dr Dorrimore. I was myself in shadow, and stood still with clenched hands and set teeth, trying to control the impulse to leap upon and strangle him. A moment later a second figure joined him and clung to his arm. It was Margaret Corray!

I cannot rightly relate what occurred. I know that I sprang forward, bent upon murder; I know that I was found in the grey of the morning, bruised and bloody, with finger marks upon my throat. I was taken to the Putnam House, where for days I lay in a delirium. All this I know, for I have been told. And of my own knowledge I know that when consciousness returned with convalescence I sent for the clerk of the hotel.

'Are Mrs Corray and her daughter still here?' I asked.

'What name did you say?'

'Corray.'

'Nobody of that name has been here.'

'I beg you will not trifle with me,' I said petulantly. 'You see that I am all right now; tell me the truth.'

'I give you my word,' he replied with evident sincerity, 'we have had no guests of that name.'

His words stupefied me. I lay for a few moments in silence; then I asked: 'Where is Dr Dorrimore?'

'He left on the morning of your fight and has not been heard of since. It was a rough deal he gave you.'

~ FIVE ~

Such are the facts of this case. Margaret Corray is now my wife. She has never seen Auburn, and during the weeks whose history as it shaped itself in my brain I have endeavoured to relate, was living at her home in Oakland, wondering where her lover was and why he did not write. The other day I saw in the Baltimore *Sun* the following paragraph:

Professor Valentine Dorrimore, the hypnotist, had a large audience last night. The lecturer, who has lived most of his life in India, gave some marvellous exhibitions of his power, hypnotising anyone who chose to submit himself to the experiment, by merely looking at him. In fact, he twice hypnotised the entire audience (reporters alone exempted), making all entertain the most extraordinary illusions. The most valuable feature of the lecture was the disclosure of the methods of the Hindu jugglers in their famous performances, familiar in the mouths of travellers. The professor declares that these thaumaturgists have acquired such skill in the art which he learned at their feet that they perform their miracles by simply throwing the 'spectators' into a state of hypnosis and telling them what to see and hear. His assertion that a peculiarly susceptible subject may be kept in the realm of the unreal for weeks, months, and even years, dominated by whatever delusions and hallucinations the operator may from time to time suggest, is a trifle disquieting.

John Bartine's Watch

A Story by a Physician

'The exact time? Good God! my friend, why do you insist? One would think – but what does it matter; it is easily bedtime – isn't that near enough? But, here, if you must set your watch, take mine and see for yourself.'

With that he detached his watch – a tremendously heavy, old-fashioned one – from the chain, and handed it to me; then turned away, and walking across the room to a shelf of books, began an examination of their backs. His agitation and evident distress surprised me; they appeared reasonless. Having set my watch by his I stepped over to where he stood and said, 'Thank you.'

As he took his timepiece and reattached it to the guard I observed that his hands were unsteady. With a tact upon which I greatly prided myself, I sauntered carelessly to the sideboard and took some brandy and water; then, begging his pardon for my thoughtlessness, asked him to have some and went back to my seat by the fire, leaving him to help himself, as was our custom. He did so and presently joined me at the hearth, as tranquil as ever.

This odd little incident occurred in my apartment, where John Bartine was passing an evening. We had dined together at the club, had come home in a cab and – in short, everything had been done in the most prosaic way; and why John Bartine should break in upon the natural and established order of things to make himself spectacular with a display of emotion, apparently for his own entertainment, I could nowise understand. The more I thought of it, while his brilliant conversational gifts were commending themselves to my inattention, the more curious I grew, and of course had no difficulty in persuading myself that my curiosity was friendly solicitude. That is the disguise that curiosity usually assumes to evade resentment. So I ruined one of the finest sentences of his disregarded monologue by cutting it short without ceremony.

'John Bartine,' I said, 'you must try to forgive me if I am wrong, but with the light that I have at present I cannot concede your right to go all to pieces when asked the time o' night. I cannot admit that it is proper to experience a mysterious reluctance to look your own watch in the face and to cherish in my presence, without explanation, painful emotions which are denied to me, and which are none of my business.'

To this ridiculous speech Bartine made no immediate reply, but sat looking gravely into the fire. Fearing that I had offended I was about to apologise and beg him to think no more about the matter, when looking me calmly in the eyes he said: 'My dear fellow, the levity of your manner does not at all disguise the hideous impudence of your demand; but happily I had already decided to tell you what you wish to know, and no manifestation of your unworthiness to hear it shall alter my decision. Be good enough to give me your attention and you shall hear all about the matter.

'This watch,' he said, 'had been in my family for three generations before it fell to me. Its original owner, for whom it was made, was my great-grandfather, Bramwell Olcott Bartine, a wealthy planter of Colonial Virginia, and as staunch a Tory as ever lay awake nights contriving new kinds of maledictions for the head of Mr Washington, and new methods of aiding and abetting good King George. One day this worthy gentleman had the deep misfortune to perform for his cause a service of capital importance which was not recognised as legitimate by those who suffered its disadvantages. It does not matter what it was, but among its minor consequences was my excellent ancestor's arrest one night in his own house by a party ` of Mr Washington's rebels. He was permitted to say farewell to his weeping family, and was then marched away into the darkness which swallowed him up for ever. Not the slenderest clue to his fate was ever found. After the war the most diligent inquiry and the offer of large rewards failed to turn up any of his captors or any fact concerning his disappearance. He had disappeared, and that was all.'

Something in Bartine's manner that was not in his words – I hardly knew what it was – prompted me to ask: 'What is your view of the matter – of the justice of it?'

'My view of it,' he flamed out, bringing his clenched hand down upon the table as if he had been in a public-house dicing with blackguards – 'my view of it is that it was a characteristically dastardly assassination by that damned traitor, Washington, and his ragamuffin rebels!'

For some minutes nothing was said: Bartine was recovering his temper, and I waited. Then I said: 'Was that all?'

'No – there was something else. A few weeks after my great-grandfather's arrest his watch was found lying on the porch at the front door of his dwelling. It was wrapped in a sheet of letter paper bearing the name of Rupert Bartine, his only son, my grandfather. I am wearing that watch.'

Bartine paused. His usually restless black eyes were staring fixedly into the grate, a point of red light in each, reflected from the glowing coals. He seemed to have forgotten me. A sudden threshing of the branches of a tree outside one of the windows, and almost at the same instant a rattle of rain against the glass, recalled him to a sense of his surroundings. A storm had risen, heralded by a single gust of wind, and in a few moments the steady plash of the water on the pavement was distinctly heard. I hardly know why I relate this incident; it seemed somehow to have a certain significance and relevancy which I am unable now to discern. It at least added an element of seriousness, almost solemnity. Bartine resumed: 'I have a singular feeling toward this watch – a kind of affection for it; I like to have it about me, though partly from its weight, and partly for a reason I shall now explain, I seldom carry it. The reason is this: Every evening when I have it with me I feel an unaccountable desire to open and consult it, even if I can think of no reason for wishing to know the time. But if I yield to it, the moment my eyes rest upon the dial I am filled with a mysterious apprehension – a sense of imminent calamity. And this is the more insupportable the nearer it is to eleven o'clock – by this watch, no matter what the actual hour may be. After the hands have registered eleven the desire to look is gone; I am entirely indifferent. Then I can consult the thing as often as I like, with no more emotion than you feel in looking at your own. Naturally I have trained myself not to look at that watch in the evening before eleven; nothing could induce me. Your insistence this evening upset me a trifle. I felt very much as I suppose an opium-eater might feel if his yearning for his special and particular kind of hell were reinforced by opportunity and advice.

'Now that is my story, and I have told it in the interest of your trumpery science; but if on any evening hereafter you observe me wearing this damnable watch, and you have the thoughtfulness to ask me the hour, I shall beg leave to put you to the inconvenience of being knocked down.'

His humour did not amuse me. I could see that in relating his delusion he was again somewhat disturbed. His concluding smile was positively ghastly, and his eyes had resumed something more than their old restlessness; they shifted hither and thither about the room with apparent aimlessness and I fancied had taken on a wild expression, such as is sometimes observed in cases of dementia. Perhaps this was my own imagination, but at any rate I was now persuaded that my friend was afflicted with a most singular and interesting monomania. Without, I trust, any abatement of my affectionate solicitude for him as a friend, I began to regard him as a patient, rich in possibilities of profitable study. Why not? Had he not described his delusion in the interest of science? Ah, poor fellow, he was doing more for science than he knew: not only his story but himself was in evidence. I should cure him if I could, of course, but first I should make a little experiment in psychology – nay, the experiment itself might be a step in his restoration.

'That is very frank and friendly of you, Bartine,' I said cordially, 'and I'm rather proud of your confidence. It is all very odd, certainly. Do you mind showing me the watch?'

He detached it from his waistcoat, chain and all, and passed it to me without a word. The case was of gold, very thick and strong, and singularly engraved. After closely examining the dial and observing that it was nearly twelve o'clock, I opened it at the back and was interested to observe an inner case of ivory, upon which was painted a miniature portrait in that exquisite and delicate manner which was in vogue during the eighteenth century.

'Why, bless my soul!' I exclaimed, feeling a sharp artistic delight – 'how under the sun did you get that done? I thought miniature painting on ivory was a lost art.'

'That,' he replied, gravely smiling, 'is not I; it is my excellent great-grandfather, the late Bramwell Olcott Bartine, Esquire, of Virginia. He was younger then than later – about my age, in fact. It is said to resemble me; do you think so?'

'Resemble you? I should say so! Barring the costume, which I supposed you to have assumed out of compliment to the art – or for *vraisemblance*, so to say – and the no moustache, that portrait is you in every feature, line, and expression.'

No more was said at that time. Bartine took a book from the table and began reading. I heard outside the incessant plash of the rain in the street. There were occasional hurried footfalls on the sidewalks; and once a slower, heavier tread seemed to cease at my door – a policeman, I thought, seeking shelter in the doorway. The boughs of the trees tapped significantly on the window panes, as if asking for admittance. I remember it all through these years and years of a wiser, graver life.

Seeing myself unobserved, I took the old-fashioned key that dangled from the chain and quickly turned back the hands of the watch a full hour; then, closing the case, I handed Bartine his property and saw him replace it on his person.

'I think you said,' I began, with assumed carelessness, 'that after eleven the sight of the dial no longer affects you. As it is now nearly twelve' – looking at my own timepiece – 'perhaps, if you don't resent my pursuit of proof, you will look at it now.'

He smiled good-humouredly, pulled out the watch again, opened it, and instantly sprang to his feet with a cry that Heaven has not had the mercy to permit me to forget! His eyes, their blackness strikingly intensified by the pallor of his face, were fixed upon the watch, which he clutched in both hands. For some time he remained in that attitude without uttering another sound; then, in a voice that I should not have recognised as his, he said: 'Damn you! it is two minutes to eleven!'

I was not unprepared for some such outbreak, and without rising replied, calmly enough: 'I beg your pardon; I must have misread your watch in setting my own by it.'

He shut the case with a sharp snap and put the watch in his pocket. He looked at me and made an attempt to smile, but his lower lip quivered and he seemed unable to close his mouth. His hands, also, were shaking, and he thrust them, clenched, into the pockets of his sackcoat. The courageous spirit was manifestly endeavouring to subdue the coward body. The effort was too great; he began to sway from side to side, as from vertigo, and before I could spring from my chair to support him his knees gave way and he pitched awkwardly forward and fell upon his face. I sprang to assist him to rise; but when John Bartine rises we shall all rise. The post-mortem examination disclosed nothing; every organ was normal and sound. But when the body had been prepared for burial a faint dark circle was seen to have developed around the neck; at least I was so assured by several persons who said they saw it, but of my own knowledge I cannot say if that was true.

Nor can I set limitations to the law of heredity. I do not know that in the spiritual world a sentiment or emotion may not survive the heart that held it, and seek expression in a kindred life, ages removed. Surely, if I were to guess at the fate of Bramwell Olcott Bartine, I should guess that he was hanged at eleven o'clock in the evening, and that he had been allowed several hours in which to prepare for the change.

As to John Bartine, my friend, my patient for five minutes, and – Heaven forgive me! – my victim for eternity, there is no more to say. He is buried, and his watch with him – I saw to that. May God rest his soul in Paradise, and the soul of his Virginian ancestor, if, indeed, they are two souls.

The Dammed Thing

✥ ONE ✥

One does not always Eat what is on the Table

By the light of a tallow candle which had been placed on one end of a rough table a man was reading something written in a book. It was an old account book, greatly worn; and the writing was not, apparently, very legible, for the man sometimes held the page close to the flame of the candle to get a stronger light on it. The shadow of the book would then throw into obscurity a half of the room, darkening a number of faces and figures; for besides the reader, eight other men were present. Seven of them sat against the rough log walls, silent, motionless, and the room being small, not very far from the table. By extending an arm any one of them could have touched the eighth man, who lay on the table, face upward, partly covered by a sheet, his arms at his sides. He was dead.

The man with the book was not reading aloud, and no one spoke; all seemed to be waiting for something to occur; the dead man only was without expectation. From the blank darkness outside came in, through the aperture that served for a window, all the ever unfamiliar noises of night in the wilderness – the long nameless note of a distant coyote; the stilly pulsing thrill of tireless insects in trees; strange cries of night birds, so different from those of the birds of day; the drone of great blundering beetles, and all that mysterious chorus of small sounds that seem always to have been but half heard when they have suddenly ceased, as if conscious of an indiscretion. But nothing of all this was noted in that company; its members were not overmuch addicted to idle interest in matters of no practical importance; that was obvious in every line of their rugged faces – obvious even in the dim light of the single candle. They were evidently men of the vicinity – farmers and woodsmen.

The person reading was a trifle different; one would have said of him that he was of the world, worldly, albeit there was that in his attire which attested a certain fellowship with the organisms of his environment. His coat would hardly have passed muster in San Francisco; his foot-gear was not of urban origin, and the hat that lay by him on the floor (he was the only one uncovered) was such that if one had considered it as an article of mere personal adornment he would have missed its meaning. In countenance the man was rather prepossessing, with just a hint of sternness; though that he may have assumed or cultivated, as appropriate to one in authority. For he was a coroner. It was by virtue of his office that he had possession of the book in which he was reading; it had been found among the dead man's effects – in his cabin, where the inquest was now taking place.

When the coroner had finished reading he put the book into his breast pocket. At that moment the door was pushed open and a young man entered. He, clearly, was not of mountain birth and breeding: he was clad as those who dwell in cities. His clothing was dusty, however, as from travel. He had, in fact, been riding hard to attend the inquest.

The coroner nodded; no one else greeted him.

'We have waited for you,' said the coroner. 'It is necessary to have done with this business tonight.'

The young man smiled. 'I am sorry to have kept you,' he said. 'I went away, not to evade your summons, but to post to my newspaper an account of what I suppose I am called back to relate.'

The coroner smiled.

'The account that you posted to your newspaper,' he said, 'differs, probably, from that which you will give here under oath.'

'That,' replied the other, rather hotly and with a visible flush, 'is as you please. I used manifold paper and have a copy of what I sent. It was not written as news, for it is incredible, but as fiction. It may go as a part of my testimony under oath.'

'But you say it is incredible.'

'That is nothing to you, sir, if I also swear that it is true.'

The coroner was silent for a time, his eyes upon the floor. The men about the sides of the cabin talked in whispers, but seldom withdrew their gaze from the face of the corpse. Presently the coroner lifted his eyes and said: 'We will resume the inquest.'

The men removed their hats. The witness was sworn.

'What is your name?' the coroner asked.

'William Harker.'

'Age?'

'Twenty-seven.'

'You knew the deceased, Hugh Morgan?'

'Yes.'

'You were with him when he died?'

'Near him.'

'How did that happen – your presence, I mean?'

'I was visiting him at this place to shoot and fish. A part of my purpose, however, was to study him and his odd, solitary way of life. He seemed a good model for a character in fiction. I sometimes write stories.'

'I sometimes read them.'

'Thank you.'

'Stories in general – not yours.'

Some of the jurors laughed. Against a sombre background humour shows high lights. Soldiers in the intervals of battle laugh easily, and a jest in the death chamber conquers by surprise.

'Relate the circumstances of this man's death,' said the coroner. 'You may use any notes or memoranda that you please.'

The witness understood. Pulling a manuscript from his breast pocket he held it near the candle and turning the leaves until he found the passage that he wanted began to read.

✎ TWO ✎

What may happen in a Field of Wild Oats

' . . . The sun had hardly risen when we left the house. We were looking for quail, each with a shotgun, but we had only one dog. Morgan said that our best ground was beyond a certain ridge that he pointed out, and we crossed it by a trail through the *chaparral*. On the other side was comparatively level ground, thickly covered with wild oats. As we emerged from the *chaparral* Morgan was but a few yards in advance. Suddenly we heard, at a little distance to our right and partly in front, a noise as of some animal thrashing about in the bushes, which we could see were violently agitated.

' "We've started a deer," I said. "I wish we had brought a rifle."

'Morgan, who had stopped and was intently watching the agitated *chaparral*, said nothing, but had cocked both barrels of his gun and was holding it in readiness to aim. I thought him a trifle excited, which surprised me, for he had a reputation for exceptional coolness, even in moments of sudden and imminent peril.

' "Oh, come," I said. "You are not going to fill up a deer with quail-shot, are you?"

'Still he did not reply; but catching a sight of his face as he turned it slightly toward me I was struck by the intensity of his look. Then I understood that we had serious business in hand, and my first conjecture was that we had "jumped" a grizzly. I advanced to Morgan's side, cocking my piece as I moved.

'The bushes were now quiet and the sounds had ceased, but Morgan was as attentive to the place as before.

' "What is it? What the devil is it?" I asked.

' "That Damned Thing!" he replied, without turning his head. His voice was husky and unnatural. He trembled visibly.

'I was about to speak further, when I observed the wild oats near the place of the disturbance moving – in the most inexplicable way. I can hardly describe it. It seemed as if stirred by a streak of wind, which not only bent it, but pressed it down – crushed it so that it did not rise; and this movement was slowly prolonging itself directly toward us.

'Nothing that I had ever seen had affected me so strangely as this unfamiliar and unaccountable phenomenon, yet I am unable to recall any sense of fear. I remember – and tell it here because, singularly enough, I recollected it then – that once in looking carelessly out of an open window I momentarily mistook a small tree close at hand for one of a group of larger trees at a little distance away. It looked the same size as the others, but being more distinctly and sharply defined in mass and detail seemed out of harmony with them. It was a mere falsification of the law of aerial perspective, but it startled, almost terrified me. We so rely upon the orderly operation of familiar natural laws that any seeming suspension of them is noted as a menace to our safety, a warning of unthinkable calamity. So now the apparently causeless movement of the herbage and the slow, undeviating approach of the line of disturbance were distinctly disquieting. My companion appeared actually frightened, and I could hardly credit my senses when I saw him suddenly throw his gun to his shoulder and fire both barrels at the agitated grain! Before the smoke of the discharge had cleared away I heard a loud savage cry – a scream like that of a wild animal – and flinging his gun upon the ground Morgan sprang away and ran swiftly from the spot. At the same instant I was thrown violently to the ground by the impact of something unseen in the smoke – some soft, heavy substance that seemed thrown against me with great force.

'Before I could get upon my feet and recover my gun, which seemed to have been struck from my hands, I heard Morgan crying out as if in mortal agony, and mingling with his cries were such hoarse, savage sounds as one hears from fighting dogs. Inexpressibly terrified, I struggled to my feet and looked in the direction of Morgan's retreat; and may Heaven in mercy spare me from another sight like that! At a distance of less than thirty yards was my friend, down upon one knee, his head thrown back at a frightful angle, hatless, his long hair in disorder and his whole body in violent movement from side to side, backward and forward. His right arm was lifted and seemed to lack the hand – at least, I could see none. The other arm was invisible. At times, as my memory now reports this extraordinary scene, I could discern but a part of his body; it was as if he had been partly blotted out – I cannot otherwise express it – then a shifting of his position would bring it all into view again.

'All this must have occurred within a few seconds, yet in that time Morgan assumed all the postures of a determined wrestler vanquished by superior weight and strength. I saw nothing but him, and him not always distinctly. During the entire incident his shouts and curses were heard, as if through an enveloping uproar of such sounds of rage and fury as I had never heard from the throat of man or brute!

'For a moment only I stood irresolute, then throwing down my gun I ran forward to my friend's assistance. I had a vague belief that he was suffering from a fit, or some form of convulsion. Before I could reach his side he was down and quiet. All sounds had ceased, but with a feeling of such terror as even these awful events had not inspired I now saw again the mysterious movement of the wild oats, prolonging itself from the trampled area about the prostrate man toward the edge of a wood. It was only when it had reached the wood that I was able to withdraw my eyes and look at my companion. He was dead.'

☙ THREE ❧

A Man though Naked may be in Rags

The coroner rose from his seat and stood beside the dead man. Lifting an edge of the sheet he pulled it away, exposing the entire body, altogether naked and showing in the candle-light a clay-like yellow. It had, however, broad maculations of bluish black, obviously caused by extravasated blood from contusions. The chest and sides looked as if they had been beaten with a bludgeon. There were dreadful lacerations; the skin was torn in strips and shreds.

The coroner moved round to the end of the table and undid a silk handkerchief which had been passed under the chin and knotted on the top of the head. When the handkerchief was drawn away it exposed what had been the throat. Some of the jurors who had risen to get a better view repented their curiosity and turned away their faces. Witness Harker went to the open window and leaned out across the sill, faint and sick. Dropping the handkerchief upon the dead man's neck the coroner stepped to an angle of the room and from a pile of clothing produced one garment after another, each of which he held up a moment for inspection. All were torn, and stiff with blood. The jurors did not make a closer inspection. They seemed rather uninterested. They had, in truth, seen all this before; the only thing that was new to them being Harker's testimony.

'Gentlemen,' the coroner said, 'we have no more evidence, I think. Your duty has been already explained to you; if there is nothing you wish to ask you may go outside and consider your verdict.'

The foreman rose – a tall, bearded man of sixty, coarsely clad.

'I should like to ask one question, Mr Coroner,' he said. 'What asylum did this yer last witness escape from?'

'Mr Harker,' said the coroner gravely and tranquilly, 'from what asylum did you last escape?'

Harker flushed crimson again, but said nothing, and the seven jurors rose and solemnly filed out of the cabin.

'If you have done insulting me, sir,' said Harker, as soon as he and the officer were left alone with the dead man, 'I suppose I am at liberty to go?'

'Yes.'

Harker started to leave, but paused, with his hand on the door latch. The habit of his profession was strong in him – stronger than his sense of personal dignity. He turned about and said:

'The book that you have there – I recognise it as Morgan's diary. You seemed greatly interested in it; you read in it while I was testifying. May I see it? The public would like – '

'The book will cut no figure in this matter,' replied the official, slipping it into his coat pocket; 'all the entries in it were made before the writer's death.'

As Harker passed out of the house the jury re-entered and stood about the table, on which the now covered corpse showed under the sheet with sharp definition. The foreman seated himself near the candle, produced from his breast pocket a pencil and scrap of paper and wrote rather laboriously the following verdict, which with various degrees of effort all signed: 'We, the jury, do find that the remains come to their death at the hands of a mountain lion, but some of us thinks, all the same, they had fits.'

✥ FOUR ✥

An Explanation from the Tomb

In the diary of the late Hugh Morgan are certain interesting entries having, possibly, a scientific value as suggestions. At the inquest upon his body the book was not put in evidence; possibly the coroner thought it not worthwhile to confuse the jury. The date of the first of the entries mentioned cannot be ascertained; the upper part of the leaf is torn away; the part of the entry remaining follows:

. . . would run in a half-circle, keeping his head turned always toward the centre, and again he would stand still, barking furiously. At last he ran away into the brush as fast as he could go. I thought at first that he had gone mad, but on returning to the house found no other alteration in his manner than what was obviously due to fear of punishment.

Can a dog see with his nose? Do odours impress some cerebral centre with images of the thing that emitted them? . . .

SEPTEMBER 2 – Looking at the stars last night as they rose above the crest of the ridge east of the house, I observed them successively disappear – from left to right. Each was eclipsed but an instant, and only a few at the same time, but along the entire length of the ridge all that were within a degree or two of the crest were blotted out. It was as if something had passed along between me and them; but I could not see it, and the stars were not thick enough to define its outline. Ugh! don't like this.' . . .

Several weeks' entries are missing, three leaves being torn from the book.

SEPTEMBER 27 – It has been about here again – I find evidences of its presence every day. I watched again all last night in the same cover, gun in hand, double-charged with buckshot. In the morning the fresh footprints were there, as before. Yet I would have sworn that I did not sleep – indeed, I hardly sleep at all. It is terrible, insupportable! If these amazing experiences are real I shall go mad; if they are fanciful I am mad already.

OCTOBER 3 – I shall not go – it shall not drive me away. No, this is *my* house, *my* land. God hates a coward . . .

OCTOBER 5 – I can stand it no longer; I have invited Harker to pass a few weeks with me – he has a level head. I can judge from his manner if he thinks me mad.

OCTOBER 7 – I have the solution of the mystery; it came to me last night – suddenly, as by revelation. How simple – how terribly simple!

There are sounds that we cannot hear. At either end of the scale are notes that stir no chord of that imperfect instrument, the human ear. They are too high or too grave. I have observed a flock of blackbirds occupying an entire tree-top – the tops of several trees – and all in full song. Suddenly – in a moment – at absolutely the same instant – all spring into the air and fly away. How? They could not all see one another – whole tree-tops intervened. At no point could a leader have been visible to all. There must have been a signal of warning or command, high and shrill above the din, but by me unheard. I have observed, too, the same simultaneous flight when all were silent, among not only blackbirds, but other birds – quail, for example, widely separated by bushes – even on opposite sides of a hill.

It is known to seamen that a school of whales basking or sporting on the surface of the ocean, miles apart, with the convexity of the earth between, will sometimes dive at the same instant – all gone out of sight in a moment. The signal has been sounded – too grave for the ear of the sailor at the masthead and his comrades on the deck – who nevertheless feel its vibrations in the ship as the stones of a cathedral are stirred by the bass of the organ.

As with sounds, so with colours. At each end of the solar spectrum the chemist can detect the presence of what are known as 'actinic' rays. They represent colours – integral colours in the composition of light – which we are unable to discern. The human eye is an imperfect instrument; its range is but a few octaves of the real 'chromatic scale'. I am not mad; here are colours that we cannot see.

And, God help me! the Damned Thing is of such a colour!

Haïta the Shepherd

In the heart of Haïta the illusions of youth had not been supplanted by those of age and experience. His thoughts were pure and pleasant, for his life was simple and his soul devoid of ambition. He rose with the sun and went forth to pray at the shrine of Hastur, the god of shepherds, who heard and was pleased. After performance of this pious rite Haïta unbarred the gate of the fold and with a cheerful mind drove his flock afield, eating his morning meal of curds and oat cake as he went, occasionally pausing to add a few berries, cold with dew, or to drink of the waters that came away from the hills to join the stream in the middle of the valley and be borne along with it, he knew not whither.

During the long summer day, as his sheep cropped the good grass which the gods had made to grow for them, or lay with their forelegs doubled under their breasts and chewed the cud, Haïta, reclining in the shadow of a tree, or sitting upon a rock, played so sweet music upon his reed pipe that sometimes from the corner of his eye he got accidental glimpses of the minor sylvan deities, leaning forward out of the copse to hear; but if he looked at them directly they vanished. From this – for he must be thinking if he would not turn into one of his own sheep – he drew the solemn inference that happiness may come if not sought, but if looked for will never be seen; for next to the favour of Hastur, who never disclosed himself, Haïta most valued the friendly interest of his neighbours, the shy immortals of the wood and stream. At nightfall he drove his flock back to the fold, saw that the gate was secure and retired to his cave for refreshment and for dreams.

So passed his life, one day like another, save when the storms uttered the wrath of an offended god. Then Haïta cowered in his cave, his face hidden in his hands, and prayed that he alone might be punished for his sins and the world saved from destruction. Sometimes when there was a great rain, and the stream came out of its banks, compelling him to urge his terrified flock to the uplands, he interceded for the people in the cities which he had been told lay in the plain beyond the two blue hills forming the gateway of his valley.

'It is kind of thee, O Hastur,' so he prayed, 'to give me mountains so near to my dwelling and my fold that I and my sheep can escape the angry torrents; but the rest of the world thou must thyself deliver in some way that I know not of, or I will no longer worship thee.'

And Hastur, knowing that Haïta was a youth who kept his word, spared the cities and turned the waters into the sea.

So he had lived since he could remember. He could not rightly conceive any other mode of existence. The holy hermit who dwelt at the head of the valley, a full hour's journey away, from whom he had heard the tale of the great cities where dwelt people – poor souls! – who had no sheep, gave him no knowledge of that early time, when, so he reasoned, he must have been small and helpless like a lamb.

It was through thinking on these mysteries and marvels, and on that horrible change to silence and decay which he felt sure must sometime come to him, as he had seen it come to so many of his flock – as it came to all living things except the birds – that Haïta first became conscious how miserable and hopeless was his lot.

'It is necessary,' he said, 'that I know whence and how I came; for how can one perform his duties unless able to judge what they are by the way in which he was entrusted with them? And what contentment can I have when I know not how long it is going to last? Perhaps before another sun I may be changed, and then what will become of the sheep? What, indeed, will have become of me?'

Pondering these things Haïta became melancholy and morose. He no longer spoke cheerfully to his flock, nor ran with alacrity to the shrine of Hastur. In every breeze he heard whispers of malign deities whose existence he now first observed. Every cloud was a portent signifying disaster, and the darkness was full of terrors. His reed pipe when applied to his lips gave out no melody, but a dismal wail; the sylvan and riparian intelligences no longer thronged the thicket-side to listen, but fled from the sound, as he knew by the stirred leaves and bent flowers. He relaxed his vigilance and many of his sheep strayed away into the hills and were lost. Those that remained became lean and ill for lack of good pasturage, for he would not seek it for them, but conducted them day after day to the same spot, through mere abstraction, while puzzling about life and death – of immortality he knew not.

One day while indulging in the gloomiest reflections he suddenly sprang from the rock upon which he sat, and with a determined gesture of the right hand exclaimed: 'I will no longer be a suppliant for knowledge which the gods withhold. Let them look to it that they do me no wrong. I will do my duty as best I can and if I err upon their own heads be it!'

Suddenly, as he spoke, a great brightness fell about him, causing him to look upward, thinking the sun had burst through a rift in the clouds; but there were no clouds. No more than an arm's length away stood a beautiful maiden. So beautiful she was that the flowers about her feet folded their petals in despair and bent their heads in token of submission; so sweet her look that the humming-birds thronged her eyes, thrusting their thirsty bills almost into them, and the wild bees were about her lips. And such was her brightness that the shadows of all objects lay divergent from her feet, turning as she moved.

Haïta was entranced. Rising, he knelt before her in adoration, and she laid her hand upon his head.

'Come,' she said in a voice that had the music of all the bells of his flock – 'come, thou art not to worship me, who am no goddess, but if thou art truthful and dutiful I will abide with thee.'

Haïta seized her hand, and stammering his joy and gratitude arose, and hand in hand they stood and smiled into each other's eyes. He gazed on her with reverence and rapture. He said: 'I pray thee, lovely maid, tell me thy name and whence and why thou comest.'

At this she laid a warning finger on her lip and began to withdraw. Her beauty underwent a visible alteration that made him shudder, he knew not why, for still she was beautiful. The landscape was darkened by a giant shadow sweeping across the valley with the speed of a vulture. In the obscurity the maiden's figure grew dim and indistinct and her voice seemed to come from a distance, as she said, in a tone of sorrowful reproach: 'Presumptuous and ungrateful youth! must I then so soon leave thee? Would nothing do but thou must at once break the eternal compact?'

Inexpressibly grieved, Haïta fell upon his knees and implored her to remain – rose and sought her in the deepening darkness – ran in circles, calling to her aloud, but all in vain. She was no longer visible, but out of the gloom he heard her voice saying: 'Nay, thou shalt not have me by seeking. Go to thy duty, faithless shepherd, or we shall never meet again.'

Night had fallen; the wolves were howling in the hills and the terrified sheep crowding about Haïta's feet. In the demands of the hour he forgot his disappointment, drove his sheep to the fold and repairing to the place of worship poured out his heart in gratitude to Hastur for permitting him to save his flock, then retired to his cave and slept.

When Haïta awoke the sun was high and shone in at the cave, illuminating it with a great glory. And there, beside him, sat the maiden. She smiled upon him with a smile that seemed the visible music of his pipe of reeds. He dared not speak, fearing to offend her as before, for he knew not what he could venture to say.

'Because,' she said, 'thou didst thy duty by the flock, and didst not forget to thank Hastur for staying the wolves of the night, I am come to thee again. Wilt thou have me for a companion?'

'Who would not have thee for ever?' replied Haïta. 'Oh! never again leave me until – until I – change and become silent and motionless.'

Haïta had no word for death.

'I wish, indeed,' he continued, 'that thou wert of my own sex, that we might wrestle and run races and so never tire of being together.'

At these words the maiden arose and passed out of the cave, and Haïta, springing from his couch of fragrant boughs to overtake and detain her, observed to his astonishment that the rain was falling and the stream in the middle of the valley had come out of its banks. The sheep were bleating in terror, for the rising waters had invaded their fold. And there was danger for the unknown cities of the distant plain.

It was many days before Haïta saw the maiden again. One day he was returning from the head of the valley, where he had gone with ewe's milk and oat cake and berries for the holy hermit, who was too old and feeble to provide himself with food.

'Poor old man!' he said aloud, as he trudged along homeward. 'I will return tomorrow and bear him on my back to my own dwelling, where I can care for him. Doubtless it is for this that Hastur has reared me all these many years, and gives me health and strength.'

As he spoke, the maiden, clad in glittering garments, met him in the path with a smile that took away his breath.

'I am come again,' she said, 'to dwell with thee if thou wilt now have me, for none else will. Thou mayest have learned wisdom, and art willing to take me as I am, nor care to know.'

Haïta threw himself at her feet. 'Beautiful being,' he cried, 'if thou wilt but deign to accept all the devotion of my heart and soul – after Hastur be served – it is thine for ever. But, alas! thou art capricious and wayward. Before tomorrow's sun I may lose thee again. Promise, I beseech thee, that however in my ignorance I may offend, thou wilt forgive and remain always with me.'

Scarcely had he finished speaking when a troop of bears came out of the hills, racing toward him with crimson mouths and fiery eyes. The maiden again vanished, and he turned and fled for his life. Nor did he stop until he was in the cot of the holy hermit, whence he had set out. Hastily barring the door against the bears he cast himself upon the ground and wept.

'My son,' said the hermit from his couch of straw, freshly gathered that morning by Haïta's hands, 'it is not like thee to weep for bears – tell me what sorrow hath befallen thee, that age may minister to the hurts of youth with such balms as it hath of its wisdom.'

Haïta told him all: how thrice he had met the radiant maid and thrice she had left him forlorn. He related minutely all that had passed between them, omitting no word of what had been said.

When he had ended, the holy hermit was a moment silent, then said: 'My son, I have attended to thy story, and I know the maiden. I have myself seen her, as have many. Know, then, that her name, which she would not even permit thee to inquire, is Happiness. Thou saidst the truth to her, that she is capricious, for she imposeth conditions that man cannot fulfil, and delinquency is punished by desertion. She cometh only when unsought, and will not be questioned. One manifestation of curiosity, one sign of doubt, one expression of misgiving, and she is away! How long didst thou have her at any time before she fled?'

'Only a single instant,' answered Haïta, blushing with shame at the confession. 'Each time I drove her away in one moment.'

'Unfortunate youth!' said the holy hermit, 'but for thine indiscretion thou mightst have had her for two.'

An Inhabitant of Carcosa

For there be divers sorts of death – some wherein the body remaineth; and in some it vanisheth quite away with the spirit. This commonly occurreth only in solitude (such is God's will) and, none seeing the end, we say the man is lost, or gone on a long journey – which indeed he hath; but sometimes it hath happened in sight of many, as abundant testimony showeth. In one kind of death the spirit also dieth, and this it hath been known to do while yet the body was in vigour for many years. Sometimes, as is veritably attested, it dieth with the body, but after a season is raised up again in that place where the body did decay.

Pondering these words of Hali (whom God rest) and questioning their full meaning, as one who, having an intimation, yet doubts if there be not something behind, other than that which he has discerned, I noted not whither I had strayed until a sudden chill wind striking my face revived in me a sense of my surroundings. I observed with astonishment that everything seemed unfamiliar. On every side of me stretched a bleak and desolate expanse of plain, covered with a tall overgrowth of sere grass, which rustled and whistled in the autumn wind with Heaven knows what mysterious and disquieting suggestion. Protruded at long intervals above it, stood strangely shaped and sombre-coloured rocks, which seemed to have an understanding with one another and to exchange looks of uncomfortable significance, as if they had reared their heads to watch the issue of some foreseen event. A few blasted trees here and there appeared as leaders in this malevolent conspiracy of silent expectation.

The day, I thought, must be far advanced, though the sun was invisible; and although sensible that the air was raw and chill my consciousness of that fact was rather mental than physical – I had no feeling of discomfort. Over all the dismal landscape a canopy of low, lead-coloured clouds hung like a visible curse. In all this there was a menace and a portent – a hint of evil, an intimation of doom. Bird, beast, or insect there was none. The wind sighed in the bare branches of the dead trees and the grey grass bent to whisper its dread secret to the earth; but no other sound nor motion broke the awful repose of that dismal place.

I observed in the herbage a number of weather-worn stones, evidently shaped with tools. They were broken, covered with moss and half sunken in the earth. Some lay prostrate, some leaned at various angles, none was vertical. They were obviously headstones of graves, though the graves themselves no longer existed as either mounds or depressions; the years had levelled all. Scattered here and there, more massive blocks showed where some pompous tomb or ambitious monument had once flung its feeble defiance at oblivion. So old seemed these relics, these vestiges of vanity and memorials of affection and piety, so battered and worn and stained – so neglected, deserted, forgotten the place, that I could not help thinking myself the discoverer of the burial-ground of a prehistoric race of men whose very name was long extinct.

Filled with these reflections, I was for sometime heedless of the sequence of my own experiences, but soon I thought, 'How came I hither?' A moment's reflection seemed to make this all clear and explain at the same time, though in a disquieting way, the singular character with which my fancy had invested all that I saw or heard. I was ill. I remembered now that I had been prostrated by a sudden fever, and that my family had told me that in my periods of delirium I had constantly cried out for liberty and air, and had been held in bed to prevent my escape out-of-doors. Now I had eluded the vigilance of my attendants and had wandered hither to – to where? I could not conjecture. Clearly I was at a considerable distance from the city where I dwelt – the ancient and famous city of Carcosa.

No signs of human life were anywhere visible nor audible; no rising smoke, no watch-dog's bark, no lowing of cattle, no shouts of children at play – nothing but that dismal burial-place, with its air of mystery and dread, due to my own disordered brain. Was I not becoming again delirious, there beyond human aid? Was it not indeed *all* an illusion of my madness? I called aloud the names of my wives and sons, reached out my hands in search of theirs, even as I walked among the crumbling stones and in the withered grass.

A noise behind me caused me to turn about. A wild animal – a lynx – was approaching. The thought came to me: If I break down here in the desert – if the fever return and I fail, this beast will be at my throat. I sprang toward it, shouting. It trotted tranquilly by within a hand's-breadth of me and disappeared behind a rock.

A moment later a man's head appeared to rise out of the ground a short distance away. He was ascending the farther slope of a low hill whose crest was hardly to be distinguished from the general level. His whole figure soon came into view against the background of grey cloud. He was half naked, half clad in skins. His hair was unkempt, his beard long and ragged. In one hand he carried a bow and arrow; the other held a blazing torch with a long trail of black smoke. He walked slowly and with caution, as if he feared falling into some open grave concealed by the tall grass. This strange apparition surprised but did not alarm, and taking such a course as to intercept him I met him almost face to face, accosting him with the familiar salutation, 'God keep you.'

He gave no heed, nor did he arrest his pace.

'Good stranger,' I continued, 'I am ill and lost. Direct me, I beseech you, to Carcosa.'

The man broke into a barbarous chant in an unknown tongue, passing on and away.

An owl on the branch of a decayed tree hooted dismally and was answered by another in the distance. Looking upward, I saw through a sudden rift in the clouds Aldebaran and the Hyades! In all this there was a hint of night – the lynx, the man with the torch, the owl. Yet I saw – I saw even the stars in absence of the darkness. I saw, but was apparently not seen nor heard. Under what awful spell did I exist?

I seated myself at the root of a great tree, seriously to consider what it were best to do. That I was mad I could no longer doubt, yet recognised a ground of doubt in the conviction. Of fever I had no trace. I had, withal, a sense of exhilaration and vigour altogether unknown to me – a feeling of mental and physical exaltation. My senses seemed all alert; I could feel the air as a ponderous substance; I could hear the silence.

A great root of the giant tree against whose trunk I leaned as I sat held enclosed in its grasp a slab of stone, a part of which protruded into a recess formed by another root. The stone was thus partly protected from the weather, though greatly decomposed. Its edges were worn round, its corners eaten away, its surface deeply furrowed and scaled. Glittering particles of mica were visible in the earth about it – vestiges of its decomposition. This stone had apparently marked the grave out of which the tree had sprung ages ago. The tree's exacting roots had robbed the grave and made the stone a prisoner.

A sudden wind pushed some dry leaves and twigs from the uppermost face of the stone; I saw the low-relief letters of an inscription and bent to read it. God in heaven! *my* name in full! – the date of *my* birth! – the date of *my* death!

A level shaft of light illuminated the whole side of the tree as I sprang to my feet in terror. The sun was rising in the rosy east. I stood between the tree and his broad red disk – no shadow darkened the trunk!

A chorus of howling wolves saluted the dawn. I saw them sitting on their haunches, singly and in groups, on the summits of irregular mounds and tumuli filling a half of my desert prospect and extending to the horizon. And then I knew that these were ruins of the ancient and famous city of Carcosa.

Such are the facts imparted to the medium Bayrolles by the spirit Hoseib Alar Robardin.

The Stranger

A man stepped out of the darkness into the little illuminated circle about our failing camp-fire and seated himself upon a rock.

'You are not the first to explore this region,' he said gravely.

Nobody controverted his statement; he was himself proof of its truth, for he was not of our party and must have been somewhere near when we camped. Moreover, he must have companions not far away; it was not a place where one would be living or travelling alone. For more than a week we had seen, besides ourselves and our animals, only such living things as rattlesnakes and horned toads. In an Arizona desert one does not long coexist with only such creatures as these: one must have pack animals, supplies, arms – 'an outfit'. And all these imply comrades. It was perhaps a doubt as to what manner of men this unceremonious stranger's comrades might be, together with something in his words interpretable as a challenge that caused every man of our half-dozen 'gentlemen adventurers' to rise to a sitting posture and lay his hand upon a weapon – an act signifying, in that time and place, a policy of expectation.

The stranger gave the matter no attention and began again to speak in the same deliberate, uninflected monotone in which he had delivered his first sentence: 'Thirty years ago Ramon Gallegos, William Shaw, George W. Kent, and Berry Davis, all of Tucson, crossed the Santa Catalina mountains and travelled due west, as nearly as the configuration of the country permitted. We were prospecting and it was our intention, if we found nothing, to push through to the Gila river at some point near Big Bend, where we understood there was a settlement. We had a good outfit, but no guide – just Ramon Gallegos, William Shaw, George W. Kent, and Berry Davis.'

The man repeated the names slowly and distinctly, as if to fix them in the memories of his audience, every member of which was now attentively observing him, but with a slackened apprehension regarding his possible companions somewhere in the darkness that seemed to

enclose us like a black wall; in the manner of this volunteer historian
was no suggestion of an unfriendly purpose. His act was rather that of a
harmless lunatic than an enemy. We were not so new to the country as
not to know that the solitary life of many a plainsman had a tendency to
develop eccentricities of conduct and character not always easily
distinguishable from mental aberration. A man is like a tree: in a forest
of his fellows he will grow as straight as his generic and individual
nature permits; alone in the open, he yields to the deforming stresses
and tortions that environ him. Some such thoughts were in my mind as
I watched the man from the shadow of my hat, pulled low to shut out
the firelight. A witless fellow, no doubt, but what could he be doing
there in the heart of a desert?

Having undertaken to tell this story, I wish that I could describe the
man's appearance; that would be a natural thing to do. Unfortunately,
and somewhat strangely, I find myself unable to do so with any degree
of confidence, for afterward no two of us agreed as to what he wore and
how he looked; and when I try to set down my own impressions they
elude me. Anyone can tell some kind of story; narration is one of the
elemental powers of the race. But the talent for description is a gift.

Nobody having broken silence the visitor went on to say: 'This
country was not then what it is now. There was not a ranch between
the Gila and the Gulf. There was a little game here and there in the
mountains, and near the infrequent water-holes grass enough to keep
our animals from starvation. If we should be so fortunate as to
encounter no Indians we might get through. But within a week the
purpose of the expedition had altered from discovery of wealth to
preservation of life. We had gone too far to go back, for what was
ahead could be no worse than what was behind; so we pushed on,
riding by night to avoid Indians and the intolerable heat, and conceal-
ing ourselves by day as best we could. Sometimes, having exhausted our
supply of wild meat and emptied our casks, we were days without food
or drink; then a water-hole or a shallow pool in the bottom of an *arroyo*
so restored our strength and sanity that we were able to shoot some of
the wild animals that sought it also. Sometimes it was a bear,
sometimes an antelope, a coyote, a cougar – that was as God pleased;
all were food.

'One morning as we skirted a mountain range, seeking a practicable
pass, we were attacked by a band of Apaches who had followed our trail
up a gulch – it is not far from here. Knowing that they outnumbered us
ten to one, they took none of their usual cowardly precautions, but
dashed upon us at a gallop, firing and yelling. Fighting was out of the

question: we urged our feeble animals up the gulch as far as there was footing for a hoof, then threw ourselves out of our saddles and took to the *chaparral* on one of the slopes, abandoning our entire outfit to the enemy. But we retained our rifles, every man – Ramon Gallegos, William Shaw, George W. Kent, and Berry Davis.'

'Same old crowd,' said the humorist of our party. He was an Eastern man, unfamiliar with the decent observances of social intercourse. A gesture of disapproval from our leader silenced him, and the stranger proceeded with his tale:

'The savages dismounted also, and some of them ran up the gulch beyond the point at which we had left it, cutting off further retreat in that direction and forcing us on up the side. Unfortunately the *chaparral* extended only a short distance up the slope, and as we came into the open ground above we took the fire of a dozen rifles; but Apaches shoot badly when in a hurry, and God so willed it that none of us fell. Twenty yards up the slope, beyond the edge of the brush, were vertical cliffs, in which, directly in front of us, was a narrow opening. Into that we ran, finding ourselves in a cavern about as large as an ordinary room in a house. Here for a time we were safe: a single man with a repeating rifle could defend the entrance against all the Apaches in the land. But against hunger and thirst we had no defence. Courage we still had, but hope was a memory.

'Not one of those Indians did we afterward see, but by the smoke and glare of their fires in the gulch we knew that by day and by night they watched with ready rifles in the edge of the bush – knew that if we made a sortie not a man of us would live to take three steps into the open. For three days, watching in turn, we held out before our suffering became insupportable. Then it was the morning of the fourth day – Ramon Gallegos said: "Señores, I know not well of the good God and what please Him. I have live without religion, and I am not acquaint with that of you. Pardon, señores, if I shock you, but for me the time is come to beat the game of the Apache."

'He knelt upon the rock floor of the cave and pressed his pistol against his temple. "Madre de Dios," he said, "comes now the soul of Ramon Gallegos."

'And so he left us – William Shaw, George W. Kent, and Berry Davis.

'I was the leader: it was for me to speak.

' "He was a brave man," I said – "he knew when to die, and how. It is foolish to go mad from thirst and fall by Apache bullets, or be skinned alive – it is in bad taste. Let us join Ramon Gallegos."

' "That is right," said William Shaw.

' "That is right," said George W. Kent.

'I straightened the limbs of Ramon Gallegos and put a handkerchief over his face. Then William Shaw said: "I should like to look like that – a little while."

'And George W. Kent said that he felt that way, too.

' "It shall be so," I said: "the red devils will wait a week. William Shaw and George W. Kent, draw and kneel."

'They did so and I stood before them.

' "Almighty God, our Father," said I.

' "Almighty God, our Father," said William Shaw.

' "Almighty God, our Father," said George W. Kent.

' "Forgive us our sins," said I.

' "Forgive us our sins," said they.

' "And receive our souls."

' "And receive our souls."

' "Amen!"

' "Amen!"

'I laid them beside Ramon Gallegos and covered their faces.'

There was a quick commotion on the opposite side of the camp-fire: one of our party had sprung to his feet, pistol in hand.

'And you!' he shouted – 'you dared to escape? – you dare to be alive? You cowardly hound, I'll send you to join them if I hang for it!'

But with the leap of a panther the captain was upon him, grasping his wrist. 'Hold it in, Sam Yountsey, hold it in!'

We were now all upon our feet – except the stranger, who sat motionless and apparently inattentive. Someone seized Yountsey's other arm.

'Captain,' I said, 'there is something wrong here. This fellow is either a lunatic or merely a liar – just a plain, everyday liar whom Yountsey has no call to kill. If this man was of that party it had five members, one of whom – probably himself – he has not named.'

'Yes,' said the captain, releasing the insurgent, who sat down, 'there is something – unusual. Years ago four dead bodies of white men, scalped and shamefully mutilated, were found about the mouth of that cave. They are buried there; I have seen the graves – we shall all see them tomorrow.'

The stranger rose, standing tall in the light of the expiring fire, which in our breathless attention to his story we had neglected to keep going.

'There were four,' he said – 'Ramon Gallegos, William Shaw,

George W. Kent, and Berry Davis.'

With this reiterated roll-call of the dead he walked into the darkness and we saw him no more.

At that moment one of our party, who had been on guard, strode in among us, rifle in hand and somewhat excited.

'Captain,' he said, 'for the last half-hour three men have been standing out there on the *mesa.*' He pointed in the direction taken by the stranger. 'I could see them distinctly, for the moon is up, but as they had no guns and I had them covered with mine I thought it was their move. They have made none, but, damn it! they have got on to my nerves.'

'Go back to your post, and stay till you see them again,' said the captain. 'The rest of you lie down again, or I'll kick you all into the fire.'

The sentinel obediently withdrew, swearing, and did not return. As we were arranging our blankets the fiery Yountsey said: 'I beg your pardon, Captain, but who the devil do you take them to be?'

'Ramon Gallegos, William Shaw, and George W. Kent.'

'But how about Berry Davis? I ought to have shot him.'

'Quite needless; you couldn't have made him any deader. Go to sleep.'

Wordsworth American Library

IRVING BACHELLER
Eben Holden

AMBROSE BIERCE
Can Such Things Be?

KATE CHOPIN
The Awakening

JAMES FENIMORE COOPER
The Deerslayer

STEPHEN CRANE
The Red Badge of Courage
Maggie: A Girl of the Streets

RICHARD HENRY DANA JR
Two Years Before the Mast

FREDERICK DOUGLASS
The Life and Times of
Frederick Douglass

THEODORE DREISER
Sister Carrie

BENJAMIN FRANKLIN
Autobiography of
Benjamin Franklin

ZANE GREY
Riders of the Purple Sage

EDWARD E. HALE
The Man Without a Country

NATHANIEL HAWTHORNE
The House of the Seven Gables
The Scarlet Letter

HENRY JAMES
Washington Square
The Awkward Age

JACK LONDON
The Iron Heel
Call of the Wild/White Fang

HERMAN MELVILLE
Moby Dick

HARRIET BEECHER STOWE
Uncle Tom's Cabin

MARK TWAIN
The Man That
Corrupted Hadleyburg
The Tragedy of Pudd'nhead
Wilson

HENRY DAVID THOREAU
Walden

EDITH WHARTON
Ethan Frome
The House of Mirth

OWEN WISTER
The Virginian